Rose Tinted Lenses

KATERINA HARRIS

Author's note

This book won't change your life or make you stop and think about the weight of the world. But if I have succeeded in my quest, it might just make you forget about everything else as you escape into a small town romance in Rhode Island. I hope you fall in love with my characters and struggle to pry your eyes off of the pages.

Enjoy.

Contents

Prologue

Megan Saunders is perfect.

Her blonde hair cascades down her back in loose, flawless curls, icy blue eyes sit beneath her thin, fair eyebrows, and her glass-like skin is free of blemishes. Being Cheer Captain, the most beautiful girl in school, and Student Body President, she makes it clear to her peers that it is her world and everyone else is simply living in it.

Of course, the queen bee couldn't keep her throne without being fabulously wealthy, and Megan is the daughter of one of the richest families in Rhode Island. You would never catch her without a full face of perfectly sculpted makeup or one of her many designer ensembles. In short, she is desired and admired by everyone in her presence.

Kendall Lockwood is the bestfriend.

She has wavy, auburn hair that reaches just past her shoulders, and dark, doe-eyes seated beneath her bushy eyebrows. A very freckled face, usually referred to as 'adorable', much to her dismay. Her height is one of her biggest insecurities. Standing at 5'9 and towering over the other girls in her grade.

She is intelligent and athletic; being a straight-A student and the volleyball captain, not that anyone takes any notice of these achievements. She and her brother are a part of one of the most affluent families in Rhode Island, though nothing compared to Megan's.

Stood alone you'd say Kendall is wonderful.

Stood next to Megan and you wouldn't look at her at all.

Chapter 1

Kendall could feel her brother's eyes on her as she ate her breakfast.

She whipped her head round to face her twin. "What?"

He met her gaze and snickered quietly, "What's wrong, *little one*?"

Austin called her 'little one' because - even though they were twins - he was two minutes older than her and much larger in size.

She scoffed. "It's Monday morning. Must I walk around with a beaming smile on my face for you people to be satisfied?"

Austin threw his hands up in mock surrender, "Alright, alright... didn't mean to poke the beast."

He got up from the kitchen table and took his bowl over to the sink.

"Oh, and what's with you taking Megan to school today?" Kendall asked as they grabbed their school bags and trudged out to the driveway. "Are you guys back together?"

"Something like that, why?" Austin answered with indifference.

"Weren't you making out with some red-head yesterday at the beach?"

"Yeah, what's your point?"

"Man-whore," Kendall muttered as she unlocked her car.

Austin simply rolled his eyes and hopped into his black Audi, driving down the long gravel path toward their front gates.

Kendall stood for a moment, watching him with a smirk, before ducking into her vintage red Ferrari and following him out of the driveway.

The car was a gift from her Grandfather who wasted no expense on birthdays. It took him months of searching around Europe to find the exact make and model that he wanted for her. Kendall didn't have the heart to tell him that she would have been just as pleased with a Ford. Cars were never her area of expertise. Regardless, it became her prized possession and she secretly adored the attention she received when she took it out.

It was a warm day and Kendall had put the roof down by the time she arrived at her best friend's house. Pulling into his driveway, she watched as Ethan opened his front door with his usual dazzling smile.

He had the happiest spirit she had ever encountered. Ethan was tall and buff with dark skin and blindingly white teeth. They had actually begun their friendship by chance in freshman year when Austin and Megan first began their on-again-off-again relationship. Ethan was originally Austin's best friend, and Kendall was Megan's. They gravitated towards each other in their individual solitude and clicked instantly, a fact that Kendall became infinitely grateful for as Megan began spending less time with her and more time with her twin brother.

He hopped into Kendall's car and placed a kiss on her cheek, to which she smiled in response.

"Hey, pretty girl." He said sweetly as she drove them to school.

His unrelenting positivity radiated off of him from the passenger seat, much to Kendall's dismay.

She scrunched her nose. "Ugh, why is everyone in such a chipper mood today? I was counting on you being as unenthusiastic as I am about this Monday morning."

Ethan chuckled. "No can do, babe. First day of senior year, today is a good day." He received an eye roll in response.

"Aren't you supposed to be a cheerleader? Peppy and full of life? Or did you leave your school spirit in Barbados this summer?" Ethan asked with a head tilt.

"I still have it. I just save it for occasions," Kendall countered.

"You mean like cheering for me as I annihilate the opposition on the football field?"

"Precisely. I'm the reason you win all of your games."

"Not sure if that's true."

She turned to look at him, offended.

"Don't you remember last year when you brought your freshman uniform to the game on accident? The only guy who wasn't gawking at your ass was your brother, and he was busy glaring at every guy on the field, deciding who to murder first." He laughed at the memory as Kendall flushed red with embarrassment. "Both of our teams were playing terribly and Austin lost it at half-time when he overheard some guys on the other team talking about you. I'm not even sure what they said but it was enough to land them in the emergency room." Ethan said.

"Hey, don't pin this all on my brother. If I remember correctly, they had to pry you off of punching one of those guys as well." Kendall said.

"I can't be perfectly civilised all of the time. I am only human, Kendall." He quipped.

Kendall giggled.

"Well Austin really gave me an earful that night. He was so mad at me. Just thinking about that argument gives me a headache."

"Right, I remember - you guys didn't talk for like a week. After that he made it very clear to the football team that you were *off limits* and not to be discussed, or even looked at for that matter. I honestly don't know how you put up with him sometimes."

"At this rate he is ensuring that I'll be single for life. I'm going to die a virgin." Kendall complained as they arrived in the school parking lot and gathered their things.

"Aw come on, that's not gonna happen." He assured, getting out of her car and circling it to meet her. "You might just have to lie for the first time in your life. Have a secret love affair." He muttered in a low, suggestive voice, wiggling his eyebrows.

Kendall smiled at the idea and they fell into comfortable silence as they walked towards their friends.

Megan and Austin were already lip-locked when the two arrived by the lockers where their group – mostly boys from the football team or girls from the cheerleading squad – usually waited for classes to start. They all greeted the pair, some of them coming over for hugs who hadn't seen them since before the summer.

"I'm gonna head to my locker before class, see you later, Kenny." Ethan said before heading down the hall, the other footballers hot on his tail like loyal subjects.

She smiled and then turned to what remained of the group: the cheer team and the love-struck couple who looked as though they were moments away from removing clothing.

Kendall grimaced at the sight of seeing her brother's tongue down Megan's throat. "Ugh, get a room dude."

"Get a life, little one." He mumbled in between kisses.

Megan broke the kiss, causing Austin to huff impatiently. "That's no way to talk to my *best friend*." She said sickly sweet, breaking free of his hold to turn towards Kendall.

Kendall slapped on the most convincing smile she could muster. "Hey, Megs."

Megan was wearing a cropped navy tank top with a Vivienne Westwood necklace. Her jeans sat just above her round hips, showing off her tiny waist and flat stomach. Her blond hair was in large Hollywood curls that bounced as she spoke and her makeup was done to perfection. She looked fresh out of a Calvin Klein ad.

Kendall couldn't help but compare herself to Megan, every girl compared themselves to Megan. She wanted her body, her hair, and her sweet voice.

"Hey, Kenny." Megan replied as she threw her arms around her friend to envelope her in a hug, so tight that Kendall felt herself lose circulation. "Ugh, I missed you."

The rest of the cheerleading squad stood enraptured as they watched the exchange. Kendall nicknamed them 'the sheep' as they were all a load of followers who did anything Megan told them to and conformed to every modern gender stereotype known to man. They didn't have a single thought of their own, and Kendall often felt as though her IQ was lowering just by being near them.

Austin finally chimed in, causing the two girls to break apart. "I'm gonna go and catch up with the guys. Bye beautiful," he said, giving Megan one last kiss before strutting down the hallway to his entourage.

The group of girls quickly fell into conversation, if that's what you could call the sheep hanging onto every single word that Megan said about her perfect summer travelling in Eastern Europe.

Kendall mentally face-palmed at the idea of spending the rest of the year with these air-heads she surrounded herself with. She zoned out from the group and gazed mindlessly down the hallway, simply observing the passing students without any exciting observations until her eyes landed on *him*.

Daniel Stryker.

Every teacher's worst nightmare. He skipped class so often that it was surprising he had made it to senior year. He was known for smoking under the bleachers, cursing at teachers, getting into fights (and winning), and finally for being devilishly handsome. Kendall resented his unflinching ability to charm his way out of any situation.

His dark brown hair was tousled in soft waves in an effortlessly sexy way, like he had just run his hands through it. His dark blue eyes stared straight ahead of him as students dove out of the way to avoid his line of fire.

He wore a grey t-shirt that was tight enough to show off his god-like physique, but not so tight that it looked intentional. He paired this with dark-wash jeans and black boots. His strides were long and he oozed confidence as he made his way through the hallway. As he passed Kendall, his intoxicating scent filled her senses. She held back the urge to let out an involuntary sigh.

In that moment she struggled to remember why she had hated him for so long. How could she dislike someone so... *dreamy*? She quickly snapped herself out of it and remembered how completely insufferable he could be before any drool could come out of her mouth.

Luckily the sound of the bell put an end to her thoughts. Kendall was about to head to her first class when the school speaker began to echo with the Principal's voice.

"Could Kendall Lockwood please make her way to my office immediately."

Kendall felt her breath hitch in her throat as the sheep turned to look at her with dumbfounded expressions.

Megan sniggered, amused. "Woah, looks like little Kenny has joined the dark side this year. What did you do?"

Kendall ignored the accusing tone as she tried to rack her brain for any possible reason she could be in trouble.

"I – uh – um – nothing," she stuttered. Her cheeks were growing redder by the second, "I've got to go." And with that she paced down the hallway, hoping that no one would notice how utterly terrified she was.

***

What is he doing here? What am I doing here? Kendall thought to herself as she gaped at the scene in front of her.

Principal Hawkins was sitting behind her desk looking expectantly at Kendall, waiting for her to take a seat. In front of her desk sat two chairs side by side. The one on the right was empty, and seated on the left was none other than Daniel Stryker, slumped in the chair looking bored out of his mind.

"Take a seat, Miss Lockwood," the Principal said.

Kendall slowly lowered herself into the seat beside Daniel and tried to ignore his masculine scent that was dismantling her train of thought by the second.

"You're probably wondering why I asked you here, Kendall."

"Yes."

"You're not in trouble." Miss Hawkins said. Kendall released a breath she didn't know she had been holding.

"I do, however, need a favour concerning Mr Stryker here."

This made Kendall more confused than ever. *What could she possibly help the Principal with that concerned Daniel?*

"As you may know, Daniel is not one of our most... *motivated* students." Miss Hawkins said.

Daniel remained completely silent.

"Kendall, you are the top of your class with every chance of attending an Ivy league college next fall. With that being said, I have changed his class schedule to be exactly like yours so that you can be his chaperone and tutor for the rest of the year." She said, with a tone that would suggest Kendall should be jumping for joy. However, Kendall could only stare dumbfounded at the Principal, waiting for her to elaborate.

Daniel finally spoke up. "I would like to put it out there that I did not agree to this." His low husky voice made Kendall's stomach flutter excitedly.

"Quiet, Daniel!" Miss Hawkins scolded.

Kendall could see him roll his eyes in her periphery.

"Anyway, as I was saying... You will be going with him to all of his classes to make sure he is in attendance for all of them, you will also be seated next to him in all of these classes so that you can ensure that he is paying attention, and you will be tutoring him for three hours a week in your own time."

Kendall was beginning to grow impatient with the commands being thrown at her. "With all due respect, Principal Hawkins, I'm struggling to see why I should be punished for his lack of competence." Kendall said.

Daniel chuckled at the obvious dig. "Come on, *Princess*, don't be like that," he cooed sarcastically.

Kendall scoffed at the pet-name and turned back to face Miss Hawkins, who was trying to recover the situation.

"Kendall, this is not a punishment. Teaching Daniel will help with your own studying as well, and it will also help get that shiny letter of recommendation from me for your college applications."

She couldn't believe what she was hearing. She had been a grade-A student with outstanding behaviour and attendance, but to get a letter of recommendation she had to chaperone a delinquent? She was being blackmailed and she was less than thrilled about it.

Miss Hawkins noticed her reluctance and quickly added. "I wonder how good a week of detention would look on your transcript, Miss Lockwood."

"You're threatening me with detention?"

"I'm merely *suggesting* that you do what I say," Miss Hawkins replied, aggravatingly calm.

Kendall could feel her fists clenching. There was no escape.

"Now, off to class, both of you. Here is a note to excuse your lateness to AP anatomy." She offered Kendall a yellow slip of paper and a tight smile.

Kendall took the paper and stormed out of the office with Daniel strolling behind her, struggling to contain his amusement.

Senior year was off to a great start.

Chapter 2

K endall swallowed her pride and decided to make the best of the situation. Either way it had to be done, she figured, so she may as well approach it with an open mind. In any case, he might not be as intolerable as she remembered. And a bit of eye candy, she told herself, would liven up the more boring subjects.

"We are already super late, so let's get to class," Kendall said frantically, turning to face Daniel.

He crossed his arms across his chest, and his biceps appeared to double in size. Kendall forced her eyes to meet his.

"Yeah, you should probably do that," he said, and turned towards the school exit.

It was then she remembered exactly why she hated him.

"Excuse me, but that means you as well." Kendall jogged after him and turned to face him, hands on hips.

He chuckled at her attempts at intimidation. "You're cute when you're bossy, Princess."

"Don't call me that." She snapped.

"Does it bother you?" He raised his eyebrows.

"Obviously."

"Well then, *Princess*, I don't think I will stop." Daniel smirked.

'I walked right into that one,' she thought.

"Well, this has been fun, but I really have to be going now," he said, trying to walk around her.

"No! You are coming with me to class and you are going to sit and pay attention!" Kendall said sternly, blocking his path and prodding at his very solid chest.

He raised his hand and lowered her finger, visibly enjoying her outburst. "And why would I do that?"

She folded her arms and raised her eyebrows. "For an education."

His laugh resonated round the empty hallway.

"Yeah, no thank you," he sneered.

She ran a hand through her hair in frustration. "Ok, what *do* you want?"

He raised an eyebrow.

"What can I do to make you go to all your classes and tutoring sessions?"

"*Anything*?" he asked. A shiver went down her spine.

'Stop reacting,' she scolded herself. 'He is not sexy, he's annoying'

She immediately realised what he'd meant and was scandalised.

"Within reason, Daniel," she said. "I actually wouldn't touch you with a ten-foot pole."

His smirk grew wider as he chuckled and crossed his arms. "I really had you down as a good liar. I guess I was wrong."

Her retort was on the tip of her tongue, but he beat her to it. "Your dirty mind jumped the gun. I wouldn't touch *you* with a ten-foot pole either."

Kendall fought the urge to stamp her foot. How was it that just half an hour ago, she had actually thought he might be a half decent human being?

She ran a hand through her silky brown hair and sighed. "Look, I know you'd rather be anywhere than in class right now and this all seems like a big waste of time. But for me, this is the difference between getting into college or not.

"I worked solidly all through high school to get straight As. I maintained perfect behaviour and attendance records. I cannot get a week's detention and I deserve that letter of recommendation. So please, just tell me what I have to do to get you to cooperate."

She noted a hint of sympathy, then the corner of his mouth stretched into a smirk. "Did I just reduce *the* Kendall Lockwood to begging?"

Her face fell. "Fine, do whatever you want, Daniel. I didn't believe you were the bad guy everyone says you are, but now I'm starting to get it." She turned her back on him and made her way to class.

Her calling him a '*bad guy*' bothered him. He hated the assumption that he was a *bad guy* just because school wasn't his main priority, that he had the occasional fight and the odd cigarette. He liked knowing his peers feared him. But something in him wanted Kendall to think differently.

And he didn't want to ruin her future just because his was a lost cause.

Daniel pondered as she walked off. There was something he needed, but the thought of asking for it made him feel like a complete loser.

He released a breath he hadn't known he'd been holding. "Wait," he said abruptly.

She turned to face him.

He shoved his hands in his jeans pockets and walked towards her. "There might be something you can do for me."

She couldn't believe her eyes. *Was Daniel nervous?*

"Go on," she said, intrigued.

He looked around awkwardly.

"I need you to pretend to my parents that you're my girlfriend," he blurted.

She stared at him, speechless.

Seeing her shocked reaction, Daniel immediately regretted bringing it up. "Forget it," he muttered and turned towards the school's exit.

She reached for his arm, trying to ignore the feel of his bicep in her hand.

"Wait, just explain it a little more," she said encouragingly.

Reluctantly he turned back. "Look, my parents aren't too impressed with me at the moment and all my mother talks about is how she hates me bringing different girls home all the time. She wants me to settle down with a nice girl.

"I'm almost certain if they believed you were my girlfriend they'd get off my case."

Daniel looked expectantly at Kendall.

Her blank expression gave nothing away.

"Why me? Why would your parents get off your back if they thought you were dating me?" she asked, genuinely curious.

"Are you crazy? Every parent in town wants you on their son's arm," he said as if it was completely obvious.

She couldn't understand why that could possibly be the case. "But why?"

"You're from one of the richest and most well-respected families in the state, you get good grades and do extra-curriculars, and you have a perfect reputation. Don't be coy."

She had no idea she was known for anything in this town, especially for such positive things. She felt momentarily warm and fuzzy.

"Well, I can't argue with you there," she said, feigning confidence.

"Ok fine," she agreed. "What would I actually have to do?"

"My sister's getting married in a month, so that can be your debut as my girlfriend. Until then we'll spend time getting to know one other and come up with a couple believable fake stories to tell my parents. That shouldn't be hard considering the amount of time we're being forced to spend together."

"Okay, this shouldn't be too hard right?" she asked hopefully.

"It'll be easy."

"Great, so we have a deal. Now it's time to do your part by coming to class," she said firmly. She walked briskly off with him trudging reluctantly behind her.

Chapter 3

Ap anatomy had gone smoothly in Kendall's opinion. She'd got her head down for the final 30 minutes of the lesson whilst Daniel stared out of the window.

She would've preferred had he paid attention and taken some notes, but she was glad he hadn't bugged her.

Second period was English and she all but dragged him into the classroom and pushed him into his seat. It was no secret that Daniel and Mr Belling, who taught English, were not overly fond of one another. Daniel tested his patience and Mr Belling never hid his distaste for Daniel.

"Mr Stryker." Mr Belling's tone was overly patronising, "I haven't seen you in an English class since September of last year."

Daniel looked blankly back and said nothing.

"Do you recall lighting a cigarette in my class and walking out with the words, 'F you and F English. I already speak the language.'"

Daniel's jaw clenched and his fists balled up so tight you could see the white of his knuckles.

He leapt up ready to walk out, but Kendall grabbed his arm and whispered firmly, "Don't."

Daniel paused.

"Don't let him win."

That was all that was needed and he let her pull him back into his seat.

Kendall spotted Megan with a couple of the sheep a few rows in front. Megan was staring, looking from one to the other, clearly confused by them sitting together. Kendall shrugged, not having the energy to get into it.

The lesson still had 20 minutes to run and Daniel spent them texting on his phone under the table.

Kendall's patience was growing thin.

"Will you pay attention!" she whisper-shouted.

He lifted his head lazily. "I am, Princess. Don't worry." He returned his attention to his phone.

She huffed loudly and smacked his arm. "Pay attention!"

He chuckled at her angry expression and said, patronisingly. "Yes, *your highness.*"

"Mr Stryker." The teacher shouted.

Daniel rolled his eyes. "Mhm?"

"You seem to be distracting my star student."

Daniel chuckled disbelievingly.

"You think this is funny, young man?" Mr Belling said, even louder.

Daniel leaned over to whisper in Kendall's ear. "Bathroom break." And he walked out of the classroom, leaving Mr Belling spluttering angrily.

The rest of the class were chuckling but Kendall was far from amused.

She excused herself and went to find Daniel.

She knew exactly where he would be. It was where everyone went for a smoke. And there he was, as she knew he would be, under the bleachers.

But as she turned the corner, she saw that he was not alone. To her horror she recognised Blake Davis and Kai Matthews, Daniel's trouble making best friends.

Kai was tall and lean with a buzzcut that he surprisingly suited. He was lightly tanned and had piercing green eyes. Blake was intimidatingly even taller, at around six foot six inches. He had light brown skin and did his hair in short braids. His eyes were dark and mysterious. Kai was the more talkative of the pair. Kendall wasn't even sure she'd ever heard Blake speak.

The two others there, she had never seen in her life. But they looked like bad news.

"What the hell, Daniel?!" she said as she approached the group.

Every head snapped in her direction. The two guys she didn't recognise smirked as they looked her up and down. Daniel noticed the boys' expressions and quickly stepped between her and them, as a protective shield.

"Kendall, you need to leave," he said firmly. He took her arms and shuffled her back, around the corner and out of sight.

She shook him off, resisting his efforts. "No Daniel," she shouted furiously, "You need to come back to class and I'm not leaving until you do."

"Who's your friend, Danny?" a voice called from behind.

"Yeah, don't keep her all to yourself," another voice chuckled.

Daniel whipped round and glared at the boys' amused grins. "Shut the fuck up," he spat. Kendall flinched at his harsh tone.

She didn't get to see the boys' reactions. Daniel began dragging her away but his stride was much bigger than hers and she had to jog to keep up.

"Daniel, let go of me!" she demanded.

He ignored her and maintained his grip.

"Daniel let go, please," she pleaded.

He stopped, let go of her arm and spun round to face her. "You shouldn't have come. Those two guys are nothing but trouble for girls like you," he said miserably.

She scoffed. "No shit, do they even go to this school?"

His silence was all the answer she needed.

"You didn't exactly give me a choice when you left the class," she said accusingly.

His blank expression didn't falter. "Belling was being an ass."

"I don't care. Don't do that again!"

"Or what, Princess?" he smirked.

She sighed. "You are not holding up your end of the deal here, Daniel. You have to come to class and pay attention, that's all. I know Belling was being unfair but he does it because you make it so easy for him.

"Now we are going to go back to class. You will apologise and pay attention for the rest of the day *and* we will have a tutoring session after school."

He hated that she was right. He hated even more that he couldn't deny how adorable she was when she was bossy.

"Fine," he said.

***

At last it was lunchtime and Kendall couldn't have been more relieved to see the cafeteria.

The morning classes had gone well with Daniel paying attention as he had agreed. Kendall had been receiving stares from the sheep all morning so she was expecting a lot of questions when she and Daniel went their separate ways to their lunch tables.

As always, Megan was sitting on Austin's lap. The sheep were gathered round, listening intently to her every word. The football team was scattered amongst them talking about god knows what and occasionally flirting with the sheep.

Kendall noticed Ethan talking animatedly with Jane, one of the more annoying sheep. Kendall tapped Jane's shoulder and made a hand signal for her to move. The sheep flushed and did as she was told, moving to the other side of the table. Kendall plopped down happily next to a not very impressed Ethan.

"Did you have to do that?" he said grumpily.

Kendall flashed him an innocent smile. "Where else would I sit?"

"Maybe with Dan Stryker?" Megan piped up.

Kendall flushed as every head turned to face her. She noted her brother looking particularly invested in the turn the conversation had taken.

Megan giggled, "Or maybe on him since you've been so cosy with him all morning."

This prompted chuckles from everyone at the table except Austin who looked angry.

"What's Megan talking about?" he said, trying to stay calm.

Before Kendall could speak, Megan got there first.

"They've been sitting together in every class this morning, not to mention walking to classes together." She said happily, Kendall not missing what she was suggesting.

"She better be joking, Ken." Austin said frustrated.

"Oh but I'm not-"

"Megan, please hush." Kendall interrupted.

Megan smirked and gestured for her to explain, everyone at the table still listening.

Kendall sighed. "I'm his chaperone." She paused but everyone's expressions looked puzzled and urged her to continue. "We have the same class schedule and I have to make sure he pays attention, in addition to tutoring him outside of school hours."

Everyone seemed slightly less confused after her explanation and most of the table just nodded and resumed their previous conversations. Megan looked rather disappointed and Ethan just went back to his burger.

Austin however, still did not seem satisfied. "So not only do you have to spend a shit tonne of time with that delinquent for the rest of the year inside of school, but you have to tutor that jackass too?"

"Correct."

"I hope you know the only place you're going to be tutoring him is in the kitchen and only when I'm home." He informs, making Kendall feel slightly embarrassed.

"Stop Austin, that's not necessary." She pleaded.

Ethan chimed in. "Yeah man she's responsible, you know that." Kendall smiled at him defending her. "Besides, you really think the ice queen is gonna let him cop a feel just because you're not around?" Ethan laughed and Kendall's smile fell as she smacked him hard on the arm.

"Aw I'm just kidding, Kenny." He said pouting as he wrapped an arm around her shoulder.

Austin still didn't look pleased but she figured she'd deal with him later.

Chapter 4

"I'm bored."

Kendall had been tutoring Daniel in the school library for almost an hour. He yawned for the ninth time.

"Princess, I'm bored," he said.

She rolled her eyes. "I heard you, Daniel."

He drummed his fingers on the table and stared at her concentrating on what she was writing. He liked how serious she looked when she was concentrating. He figured he'd be seeing it a lot and that was okay with him.

"You're staring," she said, without lifting her head.

He smirked. "What are you gonna do about it?"

She huffed, placed her pen on the table and lifted her head to look at him. His smirk widened at her obvious irritation.

"Focus," she demanded.

"Come on, we've been at this for almost an hour. I think that's enough tutoring for today," he begged.

She sighed. "Fine, let's go over some stuff for the whole *fake dating thing*," she said, lowering her voice to a whisper.

He nodded. "Okay, how did we meet?"

Kendall pondered a moment. "Why not just stick to the truth, through tutoring?"

"See, I knew I picked you for a reason, always with the smart ideas. That means my parents will also think I'm actually trying at school." He beamed.

Kendall deadpanned at the last part.

His laugh was genuine and Kendall's skin tingled at the beautiful sound. "I'm kidding, I'm kidding. I'm here, aren't I?" he said.

She couldn't help but smile.

"Okay, tell me some stuff about you," she said.

He took a few moments to think before answering. "Well, um, my friends are Kai and Blake, I am 18 so I think I'm one of the oldest in our grade, I have a sister and brother called Ellen and Ben, I like weed." He smirked cheekily and Kendall rolled her eyes. "And... my favourite sport is basketball."

The last part surprised her. "Really?"

"Really, what?"

"You like basketball?"

"Yes."

"Do you play?"

"Yes."

"Not on the school team though?"

"Correct."

"Why?"

"I play on a team outside of school."

"Oh."

"Yeah."

There was a moment's silence as Kendall processed this information. "That's cool, I never knew that."

He nodded. "Your turn."

Kendall racked her brain for anything he might need to know as her fake boyfriend.

"Ok so I have a brother, Austin-"

"I already know that." He interrupted.

"Okay, stalker." She mocked, making him chuckle.

"I'm on the cheerleading squad, though you probably already know that. I am also 18 but my birthday was last week so I think you are older than me. My best friend is Ethan-" She paused as Daniel rolled his eyes.

"What?"

He put his elbow on the table and cupped his chin in his hand. "Nothing."

She looked sceptical, but continued. "Okay and I guess my favourite sport is Volleyball."

That spiked his attention. "Really?"

"Really what?"

"You like Volleyball?"

"Yes."

"Do you play?"

"Yes."

"Not on the school team though?"

"Correct."

He laughed at her reuse of his words.

"Why?"

"I play on a team outside of school."

"How come?" He seemed genuinely curious.

"Can't do Cheer and Volleyball, and Megan insists all her friends join the cheer team." As she said it Kendall realised how stupid it sounded.

He crossed his arms and leaned forward. His scent reached Kendall's side of the table and sent butterflies fluttering in her stomach.

"Do you even like Cheerleading?" he asked.

She snapped out of her daze and said seriously, "Of course." She felt she was trying to convince herself just as much as him.

He looked sceptical.

She stood up and gathered her things. "I must get going before football practice ends. I don't want my brother to get home before me and ask where I've been."

"You can't just tell him that you're tutoring me?"

She swallowed her embarrassment. "Well, I did. He didn't want me tutoring you anywhere that wasn't our kitchen when he was at home."

Daniel was not surprised. He actually laughed. "Can't say I'm shocked. Your jackass brother has never liked me."

She didn't even bother to defend her brother. "I promise it's not just you, he's like this with every guy that comes near me."

"But not Ethan," he said. Kendall noted but ignored his bitter tone.

They fell into step and headed for the school exit.

"Well, I guess he is lenient with Ethan because he's known him his whole life and he trusts him."

They exited the school and as they entered the parking lot they saw the two boys from earlier – the ones who didn't attend their school. Kendall could see that Kai and Blake were leaning against what she assumed was Daniel's car in the background.

They wore the same stupid grins as earlier. "Danny boy, here you are," one of them said. He turned to face Kendall. "And you brought the pretty thing from earlier."

Daniel felt a return of his earlier rage. He wanted to shove Kendall behind him to protect her from their hungry stares. But he knew they would only ask questions and probably want her more.

"Yeah okay, see you later," he replied as he took Kendall's arm and walked around them. He could hear them chuckling as they walked away. Daniel breathed a sigh of relief and released Kendall's arm as they reached Kai and Blake at his car.

Kendall stood awkwardly holding her books. Daniel's mouth twitched as he thought how adorable she was when she was nervous. He quickly snapped out of it when he realised Kai was grinning at his expression.

"Guys, this is my tutor. I'm sure you all already know each other's names," Daniel said.

Kai scoffed at the poor excuse of an introduction and thrust his hand towards Kendall. "Kai Matthews. Pleasure."

She held her hand out ready to shake his but instead he brought hers to his mouth and placed a gentle kiss on her smooth skin. She blushed as Daniel rolled his eyes.

"Kendall." She replied with a smile. Kai beamed and she couldn't help but like him immediately. His chipper and charming personality reminded her of Ethan. She turned to Blake, not expecting a similar response. Blake was notorious in school for being a man of very few words. Though it was rumoured that he was a secret genius who coded for the government.

He gave her a curt nod and she smiled in return.

Daniel was not impressed, but as he met her gaze his expression softened. "Don't scowl, you'll get wrinkles," she said.

He laughed and she grinned wonderingly at the genuine and beautiful smile that lit up his perfect face.

"Well, it was nice meeting you guys but I must get going." She told Kai and Blake and walked off to her car.

"Bye, Daniel," she threw over her shoulder.

"Later, Princess," he said casually and then instantly regretted it when he turned to see Kai burst into laughter.

Daniel didn't even stay to hear what he had to say but made his way to the driver's side of his Mercedes Benz.

"Princess?!" Kai blurted excitedly as he got in the passenger seat and Blake sat quietly in the back.

"Shut up." Daniel grumbled.

"And you let her call you Daniel? No one calls you that," Kai added as Daniel reversed the car and headed out of the parking lot.

"It's not a big deal, I just didn't correct her," Daniel said defensively.

Blake piped up from the backseat. "You correct everyone else."

Kai burst into another fit of laughter as Daniel took a deep breath and tried not to strangle his best-friends.

Kai's laughter abated as he looked at Daniel with puppy dog eyes. "You *love* her," Kai sang, emphasising the word 'love'.

Daniel rolled his eyes for what felt like the 10th time within the hour. "Shut the fuck up, Kai. That could never happen. Never in a million years."

Never in a million years, he thought to himself.

Chapter 5

Kendall walked through her front door and headed for the kitchen in search of the blueberry muffin she planned to devour on the couch while watching Boy Meets World.

As if she hadn't been dealt enough surprises that day, she was horrified to walk in on something that truly put the cherry on top of a perfect Monday. Megan was seated on the kitchen island with Austin standing between her legs. They were aggressively making out, their hips grinding against each other.

Kendall's hand flew to cover her eyes. "Oh my god, can you actually not!"

There were gasps and the sound of bodies separating, so she deemed it safe to remove her hand.

Megan looked annoyed at the intrusion and Austin looked flustered, to say the least.

"That's where we eat and prepare food! You have your own room you know," Kendall scolded. This always happened when they got back together, they couldn't keep their hands off of each other, never mind how inappropriate the location was.

"You could've knocked." Megan retorted sassily.

It sometimes amazed Kendall that she'd even become friends with Megan in the first place, considering how astoundingly stupid the girl constantly proved to be.

"It's my fucking kitchen and this is my fucking house, so no, I'm not gonna fucking knock." Kendall shouted, not caring in the slightest if she was being rude.

"Hey, don't shout." Austin was defending Meg, as always - like everyone does. "Why are you home almost two hours late?"

Kendall sensed an interrogation was coming, so she walked to the pantry to retrieve her muffin, then made for the door. "None of your business," she said and fled the room, cutting off his response.

***

The following morning Kendall was feeling dreadful. She knew her parents were returning that evening. That meant a family dinner, presumably with another family whose rich, spoiled son her mother would try to set her up with. *Oh how she adored her dear mother...* not.

Austin glared at her, radiating anger, as she walked into the kitchen. "What were you doing yesterday after school?" he asked accusingly.

Her head spun as she searched desperately for a believable lie.

"Why weren't you at football practice?" she asked, just as accusingly.

He looked at her as if she had grown two heads. "Extra-curriculars never run on the first day of school. You should know that, considering cheer practice wasn't on either."

"Oh, um, I was studying in the library," she said, uncertainly.

"Really?" He didn't seem convinced.

"Yes."

Austin's eyes narrowed but he nodded dismissively none the less. Despite his scepticism, he had bought it.

Kendall mentally celebrated and headed out to her car to pick up Ethan for the drive to school.

"So?" he drawled cheekily.

She knew what was coming.

"How are you and the *troublemaker* doing, hm?"

"Not another word," she warned. He held his hands up in surrender and slumped into his seat.

They fell into a comfortable silence for the remainder of the journey. By the lockers, the sheep were gathered obediently around Megan. Ethan bid farewell to Kendall and headed to his friends down the hall.

Kendall, feigning politeness, greeted Megan and her loyal sheep.

Megan's eyes lit up as though she had just remembered something. She turned eagerly to face Kendall. "I was wondering, where did you go after school yesterday that made you almost two hours late? Austin was really angry when you ran upstairs with your muffin without telling him."

Kendall fought against letting her anger show. Megan's condescending tone was infuriating.

"I was just studying here in the library. It's no big deal." She couldn't keep the bitterness out of her voice.

"Oh, I didn't mind. Austin performs best when he's angry," Megan said nonchalantly, and she twirled a lock of blonde hair around a perfectly manicured finger.

Kendall choked and started coughing like an asthmatic horse. The sheep came to her rescue, uselessly patting her back as she regained her breath.

As the coughing subsided, Kendall straightened and said disgustedly, "Please don't ever say that again."

Megan laughed and the sheep followed suit. "Woah, I'm sorry, Virgin Mary," Megan said mockingly and began cackling with her barnyard animals.

Kendall's jaw clenched so hard she was close to bursting an artery. She smiled, though she was on the verge of drop kicking each of them, one by one.

"Well, this has been fun but I've got to go," she said sourly, and headed to first period.

***

"Am I correct in thinking that you're in a bad mood?" Daniel asked, as he walked with Kendall to second period.

She supposed dramatic sighs and grumpy scowls had given away her state of mind.

"Yes," Kendall said bluntly.

"Why's that?"

She saw that he was genuinely curious. She huffed. "Megan is being more insufferable than usual, lately."

"Isn't she your best friend?" he said, confused.

Kendall grimaced at the label she couldn't seem to shed. "Not anymore. I'm hers, I guess. Ethan's my best friend."

She didn't miss Daniel's eye roll when she said Ethan's name. This wasn't the first time he had reacted like that and it bothered her.

"Why do you always do that?" she said sharply.

"Do what?" He feigned innocence.

"Whenever Ethan gets brought up, you either roll your eyes or make a snarky comment. Do you have a problem with him? Did he steal your girl or something? He is quite the ladies man."

Daniel leaned against the wall outside their classroom and looked down at her with his arms crossed. "Princess, I don't keep girls around long enough to notice if someone steals them," he said.

It was Kendall's turn to roll her eyes as she leaned back against the wall, clutching her books.

"You're such a man-whore," she said, turning her head to look up at him.

She didn't expect to be greeted by the most beautiful, lopsided grin she had ever seen. He could have been admiring a gorgeous painting, but his blue eyes were staring straight at her.

A blush crept onto her cheeks. "Quit smiling at me like that."

"Like what?" His grin widened.

Her face was red hot. "Like that." She cast her eyes to the ground to escape his captivating stare.

His grin twisted into a cocky smirk and he took a step towards her. "Why? Does it make you nervous?" He could see how flustered she was getting.

Kendall took a deep breath and forced herself to make eye contact. Surprised, she saw his face was no more than three inches from her own. His masculine scent made her head spin.

"Not at all," she said, feigning confidence.

"Liar," he smirked.

Kendall stared back, momentarily anxious. It was hard to resist the urge to inhale more of his scent.

She snapped out of her daze, remembering they were still in the school hallway. "Time for class," she squeaked and bolted into the classroom.

Daniel chuckled, thinking about how easy it had been to have an effect on her.

Chapter 6

Kendall returned home that afternoon without any great excitement. School was over, but dinner with Mother loomed hourly closer. This was her least favourite event of the month.

Mrs Lockwood was a mixture of characters in her daughter's mind - a Harvard graduate, a canny business owner, a wealthy entrepreneur, but not a mother. At least not to Kendall, who sometimes wondered why she ever had children in the first place.

Mrs Lockwood was away for weeks at a time on business trips. She'd pop back for a painful couple of days just to check all was well, before hopping back on her jet. Mr Lockwood had left home shortly after the twins were born for reasons that were never made clear. Their parents' absences had affected each of the children differently.

Austin had been the apple of his mother's eye. The only man she could trust never to leave her. She smothered him and never let him lift a finger. He had relied on her totally and grew into a spoiled, ignorant child. In his teenage years he began to acknowledge his bubble-like existence; he came to realise his father had indeed abandoned him. He blamed himself at first but trying to make sense of it all only upset him, so he accepted the situation and decided to be angry instead.

He turned to football as an outlet for his rage, which was not a bad idea since he was amazingly good at it. As for the relationship with his mother, it became more complicated as he got older. He wanted answers that she denied him. He began to see his mother as a person, rather than just his Mom. He began to see clearly that Mrs Lockwood's treatment of his sister was unfair, and that really bothered him.

He always said he was protective of his twin sister because his parents weren't there to look out for her. As a result, he took his big brother job very seriously. He knew he was too strict with Kendall sometimes, but it was his way of trying to act the way a dad would be with a daughter. That was very hard to do when you yourself had no idea what a good dad looked like.

Kendall felt she was in a state of blissful ignorance over her father's absence. She'd never met him or even known what it was like to have a father, so it wasn't like there was anything much to miss. It did bother her sometimes though, that he hadn't felt she was something worth sticking around for.

But her real issues stemmed from her mother. Mrs Lockwood made Kendall feel as though she was constantly under a microscope. It didn't matter that she was a straight A student or a well-rounded young lady; her mother wasn't interested. It was every pound Kendall gained or spot on her face that her mother noticed. She even teased Kendall for being unable to get a boyfriend and thus started inviting rich bachelors over for dinner in the hope of setting them up. She made Kendall feel like the most repulsive person on the planet. Nevertheless, and however much she wanted to stop trying to impress her, Kendall still held on to the dream that one day her mother would listen and respond with, *"I'm so proud of you, Kendall."*

She knew it was a stupid dream.

Kendall saw Austin scrolling through his phone at the kitchen table. He looked up and smiled warmly.

"Hey, little one."

Kendall rolled her eyes and headed to the pantry to grab a muffin. When she stepped back into the kitchen, she was surprised to see Austin looking at her remorsefully.

"You okay?" she said sceptically.

He sighed. "I'm really sorry for how I've been acting lately. I shouldn't have flipped out when you told me about tutoring Daniel and I trust you to study with him because I do trust you."

Kendall was taken aback. She wasn't even remotely annoyed at him so she couldn't understand what prompted him to apologise. Her heart leaped at his thoughtfulness.

"Thank you, Aussie." She pulled him in for a hug. Relief washed over her as she stood, wrapped in her brother's warm embrace. She needed as many people as possible to fight her corner when her mother arrived and it was nice to know he was there.

***

Kendall was right. Seated opposite her at the dinner table was a sweater-vest wearing, golf cart riding, cocaine sniffing, 18-year-old boy. His name was Chad... Kendall almost choked on her green beans when her mother introduced him.

Of course his name is Chad, she thought to herself.

Her mother had already insulted Kendall twice in one sentence. "Your eyes are looking dark and saggy," she said, "but at least it distracts from the weight you've gained."

She really knew how to twist the knife.

Over dinner her mother talked about her as if she were an angel. But Kendall wasn't oblivious to why she was doing it. Chad and his family were eating up her words with impressed nods. But Kendall felt humiliated as she poked her roast potato around her plate with her fork.

Once everyone's plates were empty and the housemaid had cleared the table, Mrs Lockwood came up with her worst idea yet.

"Kendall dear, take Chad upstairs and show him your room. You two can get to know each other a bit." She said this, putting on her most ladylike voice.

Kendall's face went hot and she knew she looked nervous.

"No."

Kendall thought she was the one who'd said it but quickly realised she was still staring at the table cloth in panic. It hadn't been her. It was Austin.

"Now now, Austin, leave them be," Mrs Lockwood warned.

After five minutes of bickering, it was agreed she must take Chad upstairs to her room but that the door must be left open and they could not be up there longer than 10 minutes.

Kendall was glad Austin had stepped in and she felt better about the situation knowing it would only last 10 minutes.

Chad followed Kendall up to her room. He hadn't said more than five words for the entire evening. Kendall smiled awkwardly and bobbed her head slightly. Chad looked at her, equally unsure about what to do or say.

He shoved his hands into the front pockets of his slacks. "I know this situation isn't ideal, but we can just talk if you want? Our parents are probably going to make us spend a lot of time together and it might be easier if we're friends," he finally said, looking at her with a half smile.

She breathed a sigh of relief. He had just made things a lot easier for her.

"Yeah that's a good idea. Come sit." She sat down on her bed and patted the space next to her.

Luckily, he was really easy to talk to and the conversation flowed smoothly. She felt bad for judging him so harshly earlier because he actually seemed sweet. She knew she definitely wasn't attracted to him but it was nice to have made a friend.

Chapter 7

F riday finally rolled around and Kendall could not have been more relieved. Her mother had left that morning to go to her condo in Cabo for the weekend. Knowing she wouldn't be coming home to a barrage of criticism had made Kendall feel so much lighter.

She finished her tutoring session with Daniel and they made for the school parking lot where Kai and Blake were already waiting. Blake with a girl. She was pretty with jet black hair slicked back into a flawless ponytail and perfect makeup. Kendall noted her caramel skin and hazel eyes.

Blake put his arms around the girl's neck in a hug. Kendall stared enviously, wondering if she'd ever have that.

"Why, hello nerds. How was your study date?" Kai said cheerfully, interrupting Kendall's thoughts.

Daniel rolled his eyes. "Shut up, Kai."

"Hey! Be nice or I won't bring my alcohol to your party later," Kai warned.

This sparked Kendall's interest and she looked up at Daniel. "You're throwing a party tonight?" she asked.

Daniel sighed.

Kai let out a chuckle. "You didn't invite her? After all she's doing for you?"

"Yeah, what's that about?" Kendall said as Daniel became increasingly uncomfortable under their accusing stares.

"I didn't think it was your kind of thing," Daniel said defensively.

"I party," Kendall said enthusiastically.

Daniel chuckled, there was a part of him that knew it would be a bad idea if he invited her. He was, however, smart enough to know he wasn't winning this one. He knew he would look like a complete asshole if he flat out refused to invite her.

"Ok, well then you can come," Daniel said, looking down at Kendall.

"Wow, try to contain your excitement," she said sarcastically.

Before Daniel could get another word out, Kendall walked off to her car.

"Maybe see you later," she said over her shoulder.

Daniel watched her leave for possibly a moment too long because when he looked back he saw Kai grinning at him like an idiot.

"You're crushing on your tutor?" the dark-haired girl asked bluntly.

"No Chris, I'm not," Daniel said agitatedly.

"You so are! Why else wouldn't you want her at your party?" Kai chimed in.

Daniel scoffs. "What does that have to do with anything?"

"Every guy in school has a thing for her and most of those guys will be at your party. She will turn up in one of her sexy little outfits and the guys will be stumbling over their own two feet trying to get her attention. And you know this, so you didn't invite her," Kai said with conviction.

Daniel laughs humourlessly. "Yeah, okay man. Sure."

He couldn't understand why everyone kept accusing him of crushing on her. He was certain it couldn't be further from the truth.

Maybe half-certain.

***

Kendall gave herself one last glance in the mirror, admiring her outfit. She had straightened her dark hair so it looked extra-long as it cascaded down her back. She had spent an hour doing her makeup to perfection. She didn't wear a lot of makeup but she liked to take her time with it. She wore a tight black wrap mini skirt with a strapless black top with diamonds lining the neckline. She paired the look with some small pink kitten heels and silver jewellery.

Once she was satisfied with her appearance, she headed downstairs where Megan and Austin were waiting by the front door.

"Cute outfit, Kenny!" Megan said approvingly.

"Thanks, you too," Kendall replied, not even bothering to glance at what Megan was wearing.

Austin looked conflicted at what she was wearing. "Do you have to wear that?"

Kendall huffed. "What's wrong with it?"

"It looks great but there's just not much of it and I don't want to be fighting guys off of you all night," he said.

"Then don't," Kendall said confidently and sauntered out to the car before he could reply.

Austin was the designated driver for the evening, so they picked up Ethan and headed to Daniel's house.

The party was in full swing by the time they arrived. Music was thumping and lights were flashing through the windows. Kendall stopped for a moment to admire the property. It was a large suburban family home with a lot of character and warmth. Daniel's family clearly didn't struggle for money but they didn't flaunt it either.

The smell of alcohol, weed, and sweat reached her nose the moment she stepped inside. Red solo cups were scattered over every surface, couples were lip-locked wherever she turned, and people were stumbling out of the kitchen. She assumed she'd find the alcohol in there.

The kitchen was beautifully homely and her attention was immediately drawn to the sparkling light fixture hanging over the kitchen island that was covered in assortments of alcohol and other beverages.

Ethan came up behind her, dripping in excitement. "Let's do shots!"

Kendall was never one to say no to shots with her best friend. No matter how many times it ended with bad decisions and hangovers from the depths of hell.

Five vodka shots later and Ethan was already laughing like a crazy person. The alcohol hadn't hit Kendall yet but she was excited at the prospect of the elation and confidence she knew she'd feel when it eventually did.

At last, Daniel walked into the kitchen through the French doors that led to the patio. Kai was with him and she assumed they had been smoking or something.

Daniel was wearing a black long-sleeve button up shirt with the top few buttons undone, so his silver chain was on full display. He'd paired the shirt with simple dark-wash jeans. Kendall tried her hardest not to gawk. He looked amazing. And he was oozing confidence - as usual.

He obviously knew exactly how good looking he was and that in itself made him even more irresistible.

Kai spotted Kendall and nudged Daniel who looked over at her. His confidence faltered momentarily as his eyes took her in from head to toe, pausing on her long tanned legs.

Kai beamed and walked over to give her a hug and tell her she looked gorgeous. This snapped Daniel out of his trance and he came and joined them.

"You made it," Daniel said casually as if he hadn't been undressing her with his eyes merely five seconds earlier.

Kendall nodded with a smile. "You just missed me doing shots, I told you I like to party."

Daniel chuckled. "Shame I missed that. How many have you had?"

"Five." Ethan came over and said giddily.

Daniel's expression hardened.

"Don't know how she's still so normal, I'm feeling it already," Ethan said, completely oblivious to Daniel's hostility towards him. Ethan looked down at Kendall. "Do you mind if I go mingle? Can I leave you here with your friends?"

Kendall smiled at his constant need to check in with her. "Of course, go have fun."

Ethan leaned down and gave her a peck on the cheek before heading into the living room. Kendall turned to face the two boys. Kai looked positively thrilled as he stared at Daniel, who looked positively furious.

Kai looked like an idea had struck him. He turned to Kendall. "Do you want to dance?" he asked politely.

Kendall began to feel the effects of the alcohol and suddenly dancing sounded like the best idea ever.

"Lead the way." He took her proffered hand and walked towards the living room and the makeshift dance floor. Over his shoulder, Kai saw Daniel send a warning glare.

Kai winked at him.

Chapter 8

With five shots of vodka pumping through her system, Kendall was confident enough to raise her arms above her head and move her hips to the beat of the music.

Kai was keeping a respectful distance, dancing with a contented smile on his face. Kendall however, was too tipsy to be satisfied with a respectful distance.

She moved closer, took his hands and placed them on her hips. They were now so close their chests brushed one against the other as they danced. She continued with the seductive movements of her hips and Kai looked as smug as a bug in a rug.

He appeared to be looking at someone behind her, so she swivelled round, dancing with her back against his front, his hands still firmly on her hips.

She noticed then, who he had been looking at. Daniel was standing by the door to the kitchen holding a red solo cup. Blake was talking in his ear but Daniel didn't seem to be listening. His eyes were trained on her and every movement of her body.

He was watching coldly, his jaw clenched so tight she could see the veins bulging in his neck. She wasn't sure why, but she liked it. She convinced herself he was being like that because of her, and that made her heart thump in her ears.

To add fuel to the fire, she lifted her arms above her head and behind her, running her fingers through Kai's hair and down to his neck, pulling his head closer on her shoulder.

Daniel's jaw clicked as his hands clenched into fists; he stared at her warningly. She responded with the biggest shit-eating grin ever and continued dancing confidently.

Daniel gulped down his drink, and scrunching up the cup, dropping it to the ground.

He stormed towards Kendall as Kai chuckled behind her. "Show time," he mumbled.

Daniel shoved Kai's arms away from Kendall's hips and dragged by her wrists into the kitchen

He let go and reached into the fridge for a beer.

She huffed. "What the hell was that about? Is there a reason you dragged me in here? I was a bit busy you know."

He popped the top off the beer and took a large gulp. Then, sighing, he turned casually and looked at her, just as though he hadn't been behaving like a raging maniac just moments before.

"Thought you might be done dancing for the night," he said nonchalantly.

Kendall narrowed her eyes as he took another swig of beer.

"What does that even mean? I was enjoying myself." She stamped her foot.

"Yeah, maybe a little too much," he said darkly, and downed the rest of the beer.

Before she could snap back, he opened the fridge, putting the door between him and her and began rummaging for another beer. But it wasn't easy; the fridge was stacked in a way that taking one item would have caused the lot to spill out.

Kendall spun round as she felt a tap on her shoulder. It was one of the guys from the football team, grinning at her with two cups in his hands.

"Hey, I don't think I've ever really introduced myself, I'm Brad," he said.

Kendall, taken aback by the sudden interaction, turned to see if the fridge door was still open. It was. Daniel couldn't see the pair of them.

She turned back and offered a half smile. "Hi Brad, I'm Kendall."

He laughed. "I know who you are. Here, I got you a drink." He thrust a cup towards her.

She looked down at it and smiled apologetically. "I'm okay, thanks."

Even in her tipsy state, she knew better than to accept a drink from someone she didn't know.

"Oh, come on, baby," he said confidently, and took a step towards her.

THWAK

She flinched as the fridge door slammed shut and she sensed Daniel behind her.

"You can leave my house now," Daniel commanded. Kendall couldn't see his face but she imagined it dark with anger.

Brad laughed. "It's just a drink. Chill out. Here." He tried giving it to her again.

Before Kendall's brain could compute what was happening, she was shoved out of the way and Daniel's fist met Brad's face with a painful crunch. Just the one punch sent Brad tumbling to the floor, looking borderline unconscious.

Kendall stood, startled for a moment, staring at Brad. Then she turned to Daniel.

He was breathing heavily, glaring down at Brad who scrambled off the floor and fled. All around there were gasps as the partygoers paused to watch the altercation.

Daniel glanced at Kendall, who was still completely speechless. Then he grabbed his beer and walked out of the kitchen.

***

Kendall had been chatting to Blake's girlfriend, Christina, for a decent thirty minutes in the living room. They'd sat on the sofa, giggling and gossiping like little girls. Kendall cherished it. She couldn't remember the last time she'd had a real girl-friend, one with a personality that complemented her own.

Kendall learned that Christina was in community college nearby, her family was Cuban American, she spoke fluent Spanish, and she had lived in East LA until her senior year of high school when she'd moved to Rhode Island. Chris touched on how she and Blake had got together, but emphasised that it was a story for another time.

They were seemingly pouring out their life stories to each other and it sure did make the time fly.

They were in the midst of ranking the One Direction members from favourite to least-favourite, when Kai and Daniel walked in and sat on the couch perpendicular to theirs.

They seemed to be in a heated discussion, when a girl interrupted them to bat her eyelashes at Daniel. He still seemed agitated from his conversation with Kai but instead of turning her away, he looked at

Kai and said, "I'll prove it." He then pulled the girl into his lap and smashed his lips onto hers.

Kendall felt a sharp sting in her chest, but she wasn't sure why. She didn't care. There was no way it could bother her because she simply didn't care. *Right?* She just regarded the pain as frustration with how cold Daniel had behaved earlier on.

Christina placed a comforting hand on her shoulder and looked at her. "Are you okay? Do you want to go somewhere else?"

Kendall faked a laugh. "Of course, I'm fine. It's just a little bit gross, that's all."

Meanwhile Daniel and the girl were still viciously making out. Kai sat next to them scrolling through his phone, seemingly unfazed. Then, the girl's hand landed on Daniel's crotch. He smirked, pulled her up and led her out of the room. It didn't take a genius to know what they were off to do.

Kendall suddenly wanted to go home. She exchanged numbers with Christina and bid her goodbye. She found Ethan by the staircase, flirting with some guy from the school's basketball team. Kendall rolled her eyes at his playboy ways.

He noticed her in his peripheral vision and dismissed the guy in favour of talking to his best friend. "There you are," he smiled. "Having fun?"

"I was but I'm kind of done with this now. How much longer do you want to stay?"

"I can leave now. Though we're walking home because Austin and Megan are having sex in his car," Ethan said casually.

Kendall resisted the urge to gag. "Ew, Ethan don't tell me that."

Ethan chuckled and patted her head.

"Why don't we have one dance before we go? I've been waiting for my turn with you all night," he said playfully.

Kendall smiled, took his hand and led him to the dance floor. They began to bob and sway to the song, Kendall dancing much less seductively than earlier.

Ethan always managed to pull her out of a bad mood, no matter what the cause. He twirled her around and picked her up to spin her some more as though they were dancing at a 50's danceathon. She beamed and they giggled together like toddlers on a sugar high.

After a couple of songs, they decided to call it a night. On the way to the front door, they bumped into Daniel and his evening entertainment, coming down the stairs.

The girl's hair was a mess and her eyes looked as though she'd been crying, though she wasn't looking at all miserable. Kendall realised that she must've given him head and her eyes watered. That's why Daniel looked completely normal.

Her chest tightened.

There were a few awkward moments of silence before Kendall took Ethan's hand and dragged him out of the house without a word.

Chapter 9

It was Monday and Kendall and Daniel had been ignoring each other all day. They'd been seated next to each other in every class, not saying a word. Imagine how awkward it was when it came time for their after-school tutoring session in the library, where they actually had to speak.

"Daniel, we've been over this a million times. Just focus!" Kendall snapped.

Daniel dropped his pencil and looked up at her. "Ok, what is up with you?" he said calmly, suppressing his frustration.

"Nothing," she said defensively.

"You've been ignoring me all day and for the past hour you've been biting my head off at every given opportunity," Daniel said.

Kendall grinned slyly. "Yeah, doesn't feel good, does it? To have someone be so harsh towards you when you have no idea why."

Daniel looked confused. "What?"

She was dismayed. "You were such a dick to me at your party. First you dragged me off the dance floor when I was having fun, then told me off for having too much fun, then punched some guy in front of me and then death-stared me like I had done something unforgivable. Then you stormed off and avoided me like the plague for the rest of the night!" She paused to take a breath. "I don't think it's fair to invite some-"

"I didn't invite you" he cut her off.

A pang of hurt struck her and she looked down, embarrassed.

He immediately regretted what he'd said as he saw her face drop. "I didn't mean it like tha-"

"Just finish the work sheet so we can both go home," she said bluntly before he could backpedal.

He sighed and did as she said. She was putting up a strong front as though she was completely unaffected, but Daniel saw right through it. He was familiar with that front. He'd been perfecting it his whole life.

***

Uncomfortable silences enveloped Kendall and Daniel whenever they were together the following week.

Kendall was happy that she had become really close with Christina, though. She was in a nearby community college so they hung out whenever they could.

Much as she adored Ethan, she was more excited about having a female friend, especially since Chris was so cool.

The weekend was over and she was dreading the week to come. Apart from anxiety about going through another painful week with Daniel, her mother was returning on Tuesday and had invited Chad and his family over again.

Kendall was in class, first period, but Daniel was nowhere to be seen. She almost felt relieved until the door swung open and he sauntered in. Kendall immediately felt that something was off.

As he sat down, she noticed he had a huge bruise on his cheek and both of his knuckles were split and scarred. He saw her staring at his hands so he shoved them under the table and faced forwards as if nothing was wrong.

"What happened to you?" she said, concerned.

"Nothing," he replied bluntly, still refusing to meet her gaze.

"Well, clearly something happened," she probed.

"It's none of your fucking business, okay?" he snapped, glaring back at her.

She flinched, feeling the familiar pang of hurt, but ignoring it. She didn't want him to see her walls crumble.

Engulfed in guilt, his face softened. *Why did he keep doing that, hurting her,* he asked himself. He always regretted it immediately when he saw the corners of her mouth drop and her pained expression.

***

It was Tuesday evening and dinner was finally over. However, the evening wasn't because she and Chad had once again been ordered by her mother to spend time together in her room.

This time Kendall was more relaxed. She remembered how nice and easy to talk to he'd been.

click

Her bedroom door closed shut and Chad walked towards her with a wicked grin.

Kendall's heartbeat quickened and she took a step back. "What are you doing?" she asked nervously, continuing to walk backwards.

Her back met the wall and he was right in front of her. "Don't act all innocent now," he purred, stepping even closer and boxing her in with his arms.

She was trapped.

"What are you even talking about?" She pleaded, panic evident in her voice.

"You've been sending me hints all night. Don't deny it." He inched his mouth to her neck and placed a kiss below her ear.

She squirmed. "Please stop. I haven't been hinting at anything."

He began to suck on her skin and she flinched at this disgusting, unwanted intimacy.

"Don't be a tease," he whispered in between sucking.

She brought her arms up between them and began pushing him. He grabbed her wrists so tightly that his nails dug into her skin and she had to stop herself from crying out in pain.

"Stop resisting, slut!" he ordered, and attacked her neck once more.

Kendall shook with fear at her helplessness. There was no way she could fight him off, but she knew someone who could. She just needed to get his attention.

She took a deep breath and let out an ear-splitting scream. Chad stumbled back and plugged his ears. She knew everyone downstairs would have heard her and it would only be a matter of time before Austin barged in the room and had Chad in a chokehold.

But Chad was furious. He stormed at her, pressing her with his body against the wall. She turned her head sideways to stop his lips from touching hers.

She feared he was about to force another kiss on her neck or deliver a painful blow to her gut to teach her a lesson, but just in time, the door slammed open and she heard gasps from the hall.

Chad jumped away as Kendall, shaking from head to foot, slumped to the floor, clutching her stinging wrists.

Austin sent Chad tumbling to the ground with a single punch while Mrs Lockwood from the corner of the room, barked orders at her son to stop.

Austin didn't stop. His anger issues were never far from the surface. They were always there, bubbling and ready to boil. Chad had just crossed a line that signed his death sentence if no one intervened. Punch after punch, kick after kick. Chad's eyes were rolled back in his head. Chad's mother was bawling her eye's out as her husband at last stepped in and tried his best to pry Austin off of his son. It was a losing battle until Austin saw Kendall shaking in the corner and finally surrendered.

Austin stood up, leaving Chad looking as though he had fallen down sixty flights of stairs and landed in oncoming traffic. His family scooped him up and after offering a couple of feeble apologies, took their leave. The apologies hardly compensated for the state Kendall was in. She looked like a wilted flower. Austin was cradling his sister's head in his arms, stroking her hair soothingly. She saw his knuckles were bleeding. Mrs Lockwood told him to go; she would look after her daughter herself. Austin began to resist but Kendall nodded at him and said she would be okay.

The door clicked shut leaving Kendall crumpled in a ball on the floor and her mother staring down at her daughter's tear-stained face.

Mrs Lockwood sat on the end of Kendall's bed and breathed a deep sigh. A small part of Kendall was waiting for a sincere apology from her mother for having put her in such a position. But Kendall knew from experience that her mother would shave her own head before she apologised for anything.

Her mother looked down at her, almost sadly. "Do you know what you have just done?" she whisper-shrieked. "You have just ruined *everything*!"

Kendall flinched and her lip quivered, but she looked down to hide her oncoming breakdown.

"I hope you're happy." Mrs Lockwood said flatly and exited the room without a second glance.

The moment the door slammed she felt all of the air escape her lungs as she burst into tears. She lay on her side in the foetal position as her whole body shook with despair.

Tears blocked her vision and she let the darkness consume her, sobbing for hours before exhaustion took over.

Chapter 10

Wednesday morning had been a series of blurs.

A blurry drive to school, blurry classes and blurry conversations. She had been on autopilot all morning as she counted down the minutes until the day was over.

But she didn't want to go home.

Home was where her mother was, sizzling with rage and disappointment from the previous evening.

She had volleyball practice that afternoon and she couldn't wait to fuel every negative emotion into a powerful and fulfilling practice session.

Daniel was sitting next to her in the study hall, typing away on his phone. She didn't have it in her to nudge him to do his work. She didn't even have it in her to do her own work.

Her wrists were aching and stinging no matter how many painkillers she took. The searing pain was a sharp reminder of Chad's hands roaming her body. She shivered at the thought.

Daniel looked up at her sudden movement, confused. "Are you okay?"

She flinched though there had been nothing harsh in his tone. In fact, she had never heard him sound so concerned and soft. But she had been skittish all morning, jumping and flinching at random sounds or movements. She fiddled with the sleeve of her hoodie.

"Yes, good thanks." She squeaked, then got up and walked out into the hallway. Daniel was more perplexed than ever.

Her breathing suddenly went shallow and panic engulfed her. The school doors were open and daylight shone down the corridor like a beacon. She followed the beam.

She was numb to almost every form of sound, except for Daniel's raised voice behind her.

"Slow down, what's going on?!" he shouted. She could hear from his footsteps he was gaining on her.

"Kendall, stop, god damn it!" He reached out and grabbed her wrist, spinning her round to face him.

Pain shot through her wrist and up her arm. She winced and hissed as she snatched her arm back.

His eyes widened in concern, he could see the tears threatening to spill as she cradled her wrist. He knew he hadn't held her that tightly and it dawned on him that something else was going on. Something bad.

A fiery pit formed in his stomach as he guided her into an empty classroom. He turned to face her, gently took her hand and pulled up her sleeve.

Bruises.

Black, blue and purple bruises littering her soft skin.

He took her other hand and did the same to the other wrist.

More bruises.

He looked down at her defeated expression. She couldn't even look at him.

He'd noticed she had been off all day but had assumed it had to be something to do with her period or a girl drama with Megan. Never in a million years would he have expected her to have been hiding bruises.

He tried to keep his voice calm. He didn't want to frighten her. "Who did this to you?"

"It's nothing," she said quietly.

He was consumed with rage, but refrained from yelling. "That is not nothing, Kendall. Tell me who did this to you?"

She looked up, angrily. "Oh, like how you told me all about your split knuckles and bruised cheek?" she shot back.

He huffed. "That's different."

"What's the difference?" she countered.

"The difference is you." Daniel said before he could help himself.

Kendall paused and her anger abated.

"What does that even mean?" she asked.

He sighed, swallowing his pride. "It makes sense that I would be roughed up now and then, but you... who could possibly want to hurt you?"

Her eyes widened. It was the most caring sentence she had ever heard him utter. He was showing the kind of care her parents never showed, not even after she'd been assaulted.

"Is that a hickey on your neck?" he said, his temper rising.

Her hand flew to her neck, like that wouldn't make it obvious. She grabbed her hoodie and tugged at it to cover the mark. She had concealed it with make-up that morning but inevitably, that had rubbed off.

She felt humiliated.

"What's his name?" Daniel's voice was harsh and impatient. The hickey connected the final dot that told him she had been sexually assaulted. The mere thought of it made him want to kill any man that went near her.

"Just drop it." she pleaded.

"I can't do that. Tell me his name, Kendall." he commanded. Her heart skipped a beat at the sound of her name leaving his lips for the second time- *ever*.

"You don't even know him. Besides, Austin dealt with him. He's in the emergency room as we speak," she said.

He released a breath he didn't know he was holding. "Good, that's a relief."

I'd be happier if he was six feet under, he thought to himself.

Her eyebrows furrowed. "Since when do you care anyway?"

"I may seem like a complete dick sometimes but I do care if one of my friends is hurt," he said matter-of-factly.

She raised an eyebrow. "We're friends now? Could've fooled me."

He frowned at the dig but chuckled nonetheless. "Look, I know I've been an ass lately. I'm sorry. It stops now."

"Are you sure?" she said, sceptical.

"Yes. Now can we please go back to me calling you Princess and you pretending not to like it?" he said cheekily.

She giggled and they exited the empty classroom.

It amazed her that Daniel had managed to improve her mood so drastically in just ten minutes. Suddenly, he had her laughing and feeling all fuzzy inside when she'd felt she wanted the ground to swallow her up just a few moments ago.

He made her feel wanted and safe.

She was unfamiliar with this feeling.

She liked this feeling.

Chapter 11

An envelope was there, in front Kendall. Her future, reduced to a piece of paper.

This was the letter that would tell her whether she had gotten into her dream school, Princeton University.

On top of that, she needed a full academic scholarship to ensure she would not be dependent on her mother's income. She wanted to get away from her mother and never see her ever again. For this required financial independence.

She reached out, her hand trembling, and ripped open the envelope. Holding her breath, she slid the paper out and discarded the envelope. As she opened the sheet she saw:

'We are pleased to inform you-'

"YES!" she squealed, waving her arms, excitedly.

She forced herself to sober up and continue reading.

'In addition to this, we would like to award you a full academic scholarship due to your tremendous achievements.'

Delighted and shocked, Kendall slapped her hand over her mouth. "Oh my god," she mumbled in disbelief.

Wide eyed, she still could not believe that she had actually done it. She had accomplished her lifelong dream of going to Princeton on a full academic scholarship.

After next fall she would never have to see her mother again. Kendall felt exhilarated at the sheer thought of proving to her mother that she could be such a success, she could be, and not *because* of her mother, but *in spite* of her.

Nothing could bring down her day.

***

Except maybe Megan's wrath. It was the third time that week that Kendall was skipping cheerleading practice, but she just couldn't bring herself to go.

The uniform was shorts and a sports bra, meaning her arms would be exposed and Kendall couldn't yet expose her wrists, let alone tumble on them.

Not only that, cheer had never been a real passion. She was counting down the days until she didn't have to do it anymore.

"You cannot be serious right now!" Megan shrieked, drawing a crowd in the hallway.

Kendall sighed, wanting the conversation to be over as soon as possible. "I'm injured, there's nothing I can do. You would be a bad captain to make me train on an injury."

This sparked some dark, "Ooos," from the watching students.

Megan's face flamed at the suggestion she might be in the wrong and she stomped her foot. Kendall took this as her cue to barge past and head for the library before Megan burst into flames.

Daniel was sitting in the library massaging his hands, unaware he had an audience.

Kendall giggled. "What are you doing?"

He looked up at the intrusion and dropped his hands.

He straightened up. "Just strengthening my hands for later."

Kendall sat opposite him and began laying her things out on the table. "What's later?"

"I've got a basketball game," he said.

She was momentarily surprised but then she remembered he'd said he played outside of school.

"Oh yeah, I forgot you did that. You nervous?" she asked casually.

He chuckled. "I don't get nervous, Princess."

She looked at him dumbfounded. "Everyone gets nervous, asshat."

"I know *you* do. I manage to make you nervous on a daily basis." He smirked, placing his crossed arms on the table.

She masked her embarrassment by scoffing loudly.

"Yeah, as if," she scoffed.

His laugh was genuine as smiled at her. "See, I'm even making you nervous now," he said.

She scowled and kicked his leg under the table.

He folded forwards and groaned. "Fuck, that hurt," he grunted.

Kendall smirked in triumph until she realised he was clutching his leg and groaning.

"Wait, are you okay?" she said, concerned.

"Yeah, I should be it's just a-" He tried putting pressure on it. "FUCKKKK!" He collapsed back into the chair, his face scrunched in agony.

Guilt swept over Kendall. Instinctively she got up and knelt in front of Daniel, prying his hands off his leg so she could take a look.

"Daniel, I'm so sorry. Please let me have a look at it," she begged.

He moved his hands and she realised she'd have to roll his jeans up to see the damage.

However, it occurred to her Daniel was no longer wriggling and hissing in pain; he was completely still.

Looking up through her lashes she saw he was smirking, his hands lazily behind his head. "I like you from this angle, Princess."

Humiliated, she shot to her feet. He folded over in laughter. Despite wanting to be mad at him, Kendall also wanted to drink in the melodic sound.

She plopped angrily into her seat and shot daggers at Daniel, who was biting his lip, trying to control his laughter.

They were both engulfed in laughter for the next five minutes or so, before Kendall insisted they get to work.

The next hour was spent productively, with plenty of learning to be done. Around 4:30 they packed up their stuff and headed to the parking lot.

"You should come," Daniel said out of nowhere.

She looked up at him confused, "What?"

"My game later, you should come," he insisted.

She tried to suppress the Cheshire Cat grin that threatened to overwhelm her. Daniel had a way of making her feel wanted. She didn't really care for basketball but the thought of spending another Friday night in her room watching Full house reruns made her rethink things.

She liked the idea of seeing him doing a sport. Though she'd never admit it, she also liked the idea of seeing him in basketball shorts. She loved the idea of seeing him win and watching that captivating smile stretch across his chiselled face. Her heart skipped ten beats at the thought of him winning and then running up to her, picking her up and spinning her around in a tight embrace.

She swiftly banished those thoughts and returned to earth.

"Yeah, maybe," she said nonchalantly.

He smirked and took her phone off her.

"Wha-" she sputtered.

"Relax, I'm giving you my number and texting myself so now I have yours." He handed her back her phone as they walked off towards their cars.

"I'll text you the details, hope to see you there," he said over his shoulder as he reached his car.

Butterflies fluttered in her stomach. "If I do decide to come, you'll have to come to one of my volleyball games y'know," she said loudly as she arrived at her Ferrari.

"Any opportunity to see you in booty shorts and I'm there, Princess," Daniel said, smirking, and hopped into his car.

He drove off leaving Kendall wide eyed, her mouth agape. She gulped and slowly got into her own car. The butterfly wings flapped so hard she was willing to bet they were on ecstasy!

How did he always manage to leave her feeling so happy - yet so confused?

Chapter 12

K endall zipped through the parking lot, desperately looking for a spot to park, so that she could get out and see Daniel.

She couldn't understand why she was so excited. She told herself it was because she was keen to see his ego crushed when the other team won.

That was a lie of course.

At last, she found a space and leaping from the car, jogged up to the venue entrance.

She entered the gigantic hall, trying to appear calm and collected, and scoured the room for the cheeky brunette boy she spent so much time with these days.

There was practically no one in the hall and for a moment she was concerned she'd arrived too early. It didn't look as though they'd even warmed up yet. Then she spotted him on the bleachers with his team. The moment he noticed her, he began a slow jog towards her.

He wore that gorgeous smile that was reflected in her own eyes as he arrived at where she was standing.

"You came," he said, breathless.

"I did. Am I early?" she asked, confused.

He nodded. "Yeah, but I told you to come now because I wanted you here early."

Her eyebrow lifted. "Why?"

He smirked down at her. "Well, you're pretty much a genius at everything. Thought maybe you could watch me warm up and give me a few pointers."

"You better be joking," she deadpanned.

He laughed and folded his arms across his basketball jersey. "Yeah I am. There's nothing you could teach me about this sport; there's barely anything left for coach to teach me."

"Modest too," she said, giggling.

He grinned smugly and winked. "You'll see."

He waved to her and began jogging back towards his team, who were starting their warm up. She went and leaned against the wall behind the hoop, so she could watch.

After five minutes of warm up drills, they each grabbed a ball and began doing their own rituals. Most of them were just dribbling and shooting every now and then.

Daniel dribbled the ball up the court towards the hoop in front of Kendall, pretending not to have noticed her. As he went for a lay-up his eyes darted to Kendall, as though he'd just spotted her. The ball bounced off of the hoop's ring.

"Nice hands," Kendall said, giggling.

Daniel picked up his ball and smirked. "Nice legs."

Her breath caught in her throat and her cheeks turned bright red.

Kendall was left stunned for the third time that Friday, as he jogged back towards the rest of the team.

***

The game had been going surprisingly well for Daniel; his team was in the lead and he had scored 90% of the baskets.

Kendall fixated on the game, with Kai seated next to her. He had tried talking to her multiple times but she was far too interested in watching Daniel to engage in any kind of conversation.

Half time came around and Kendall released a breath she hadn't realised she'd been holding. She had no idea she would enjoy herself this much.

Kai bumped her shoulder and she looked over to see him wiggling his eyebrows at her.

"You seem to be enjoying yourself," he said.

"Yeah, I am," she nodded.

"You seem to always enjoy yourself when you're around Daniel," he said suggestively.

"I'm just a happy person, Kai," Kendall scoffed.

"It's okay, he's the same when he's around you."

She looked at Kai inquisitively.

"Just don't tell him I told you that," he added.

"That's probably because it's not true," she said dismissively and looked away.

"It is absolutely, completely true. Is it so hard to believe that you make someone happy just by being around them? You're a really good person, Kendall. I'm sure there are plenty of people whose mood improves just from your presence. Your family perhaps? I bet they adore you and cherish your very existence." Kai stated this as though it was definitely the case.

Kendall laughed inwardly. Firstly, from hearing one of the school's most notorious bad boys using the word 'perhaps', and secondly from the assumption that her parents valued her presence even slightly. She was absolutely certain that her mother would not even bat an eye if she dropped dead. And her father hadn't even stuck around even to hold his new baby.

She didn't tell Kai that.

She never told anyone.

Chapter 13

The serotonin flooded through Kendall when Daniel scored the winning basket right on the buzzer. The audience stood and cheered.

Daniel's team-mates picked him up and carried him on their shoulders, chanting his name. Kendall allowed a huge smile to stretch across her face. She adored seeing him so happy and care-free. She wished she could see more of that side of him.

Once the celebrations calmed down, Kendall plodded down to the bleachers and over to Daniel. He beamed as he watched her approach.

"Congratulations, good game," she said nonchalantly.

He quirked a teasing eyebrow. "That's all I get? *Good game*? Come on, Princess, you were having the time of your life watching me kick ass today."

She reddened and rolled her eyes to hide her nerves. She evidently hadn't hidden her excitement very well if he'd noticed it from where he was playing on the court.

"Okay fine, I had fun watching you. You played pretty amazingly," she smiled.

He smirked and said cockily, "I think I deserve a congratulatory hug."

Kendall kept her arms to her sides. She'd never been much of a hugger.

His smirk grew and without warning he took her waist and picked her up. As he pulled towards him he spun her round, causing her arms instinctively to wrap round his neck.

Finally he put her down, but she'd been so startled she hadn't registered her feet were back on the ground and her arms remained firmly around his neck.

He chuckled. "I know you like me, Princess, but you can let go now."

Her eyes met his and widened in embarrassment, before she jumped away as though he was on fire.

He laughed louder and she crossed her arms defensively.

"You should come to the after party. It's at my place," he stated.

"You sure you want me at this one?" she said with a challenging stare.

He nodded, defeated. "Yeah, I know I was an ass at the last one but I promise that won't happen this time."

"Maybe." She said casually, trying not to seem too interested.

"Great. I'm gonna hit the showers and change. You can drive us once I'm ready," he said, and ran off to the locker rooms before she could protest.

***

The evening sky shrouded the parking lot in darkness, with only lamp posts providing some flickering light.

Kendall checked her watch for the third time in five minutes; she was growing impatient. She had never been comfortable in the dark by herself, probably because Austin almost never let that happen.

The doors to the venue finally swung open but Daniel did not walk out. It was the opposing team that walked towards her with so much confidence you'd never have guessed they'd just had their asses handed to them.

They didn't look at all friendly and Kendall wasn't one to wait around to find out. She hopped in her car and locked the doors, then peered out the window to see if they were still heading towards her. By then, they'd walked straight past her and scattered into their own cars. She breathed a sigh of relief.

Suddenly, someone knocked on her window and she felt her soul leave her body. She jumped and let out a squeal but saw with relief that it was Daniel at her window, looking very confused. She signalled for him to get in. He threw his duffle bag onto the backseat and turned to face her.

"Are you okay? You look like you've just seen a ghost," he said.

Kendall was staring speechlessly. His damp hair and black hoodie, his intoxicatingly good cologne, that was filling the car with his masculinity, she just wanted to crawl into his lap and snuggle into his hoodie.

She became aware she'd been staring for at least a minute, without saying a word.

He didn't seem to mind and his signature smirk made an appearance. "Are you checking me out, Princess?"

Kendall didn't need a mirror to know she was as red as a lobster. She scoffed and rolled her eyes to mask her embarrassment, but it clearly wasn't working. Daniel's smirk grew even wider.

"What took you so long?" she demanded.

He chuckled at her attempt to change the subject.

"Beauty like mine takes time," he said.

Kendall scoffed again. "Yeah okay, let's go."

***

They drove contentedly to Daniel's house with just the gentle sound of the radio in the background until Kendall decided it was time to put an end to the silence.

"Where were your parents tonight?" Kendall asked.

Daniel stiffened. "They were busy, out of town."

"Oh." was all Kendall could think to say in reply. She could tell he wasn't being completely truthful, but felt it wasn't her business.

They pulled into the Stryker residence and Kendall found herself thinking once again what an adorably homely property it was.

Daniel interrupted her thoughts. "What are you staring at? Come on, the party's already started."

She tried to keep up with his long strides as they made their way to the front door from where came the sound of loud, thumping music. Daniel dragged her straight into the grand kitchen and the whole room erupted in cheers as they entered. Daniel got pats on the back and congratulations left right and centre, whilst Kendall stood by with an awkward smile.

Guys began handing Daniel drinks and cheering him on as he downed them in seconds. Ten minutes later and Kendall was still watching idly as the scene in front of her unfolded. Daniel was seemingly a hopeless lightweight as the drink was having an immediate effect. To Kendall's relief, Christina appeared at her side.

"You came here together, huh?" Chris asked, waggling her eyebrows.

"In a technical sense but not in the way that you're thinking," Kendall said casually.

Chris didn't seem convinced, but nodded along nonetheless. "Well get ready, he's funny when he's wasted."

Kendall offered a half smile and turned towards Daniel. He looked sweaty and disoriented, but happier than ever. A pretty petite girl pressed herself up against his front and began tracing her fingers down his chest.

Kendall's jaw clenched. She wanted to look away and put an end to the torture, she couldn't pry her eyes off of them. Daniel smirked down at the girl then reached down to the hem of his hoodie and pulled it over his head. Kendall's throat went dry at the thought the two of them were about to start bumping uglies right there and then. But Daniel removed himself from the small girl's embrace and made his way over to Kendall, still clutching the hoodie.

A confident smirk plastered his sweaty face as he thrust the hoodie at her. She took it, sceptically.

"Wear it," he said firmly.

Kendall looked up at him confused, "Why?"

"Please, Princess," he said, pouting.

"Fine," she said and pulled it over her head.

He smiled down at her small frame, drowned in the fabric.

Suddenly someone bellowed, "Beer Pong!"

All the guys, including Daniel, and some of the girls rushed into the other room. Daniel winked at Kendall and disappeared. Her face was burning.

Chris grinned suggestively.

"What?" Kendall said innocently.

"He calls you Princess and he just winked at you after begging you to wear his hoodie for the night," Chris said accusingly.

"So?" Kendall continued to blush.

Chris deadpanned, "Are you braindead? His last name is on the back of that hoodie, he's making sure no guys go near you for the entire night."

Chapter 14

Chris and Kendall had been in their own world for the entire night.

Kendall knew she would have to drive home so she stayed sober and Chris, being the angel that she was, offered to stay sober with her.

Regardless of the lack of alcohol, they were both having a really good time. They'd been chatting and making fun of people for hours before hitting the dance floor to make fools of themselves.

Kai made his way over to the pair of them as they swayed to the beat of the music. He smirked when he saw what Kendall was wearing.

"Hey guys," he greeted them politely.

"Hello, trouble," Chris replied.

Kai's face scrunched cutely at the nickname.

"Hey, Kai," Kendall added.

Kai looked down at her. "Kendall, I love you but I cannot believe you let Daniel mark his territory on you like this." He tugged at the hoodie sleeve.

She rolled her eyes. "It's honestly nothing. Besides he's pretty drunk, I doubt he'll even remember giving it to me in the morning."

Kai and Chris giggled, knowingly.

"Sure, *Princess*," Chris drawled mockingly.

They both burst into fits of laughter whilst Kendall huffed in embarrassment.

"I'm gonna grab a water," Kendall said and fled into the kitchen, wanting nothing more than for that conversation to be over.

She made a beeline for the fridge, not looking around to see who else was in the kitchen.

She was frantically searching the fridge when two large arms enveloped her waist and she was pulled back into the stranger's body. She would've elbowed the culprit in the gut immediately if it weren't for Daniel's masculine scent filling her senses, and she could see his signature rings on his large veiny hands.

Even so, she was alarmed.

Daniel was nuzzling her neck and she felt soft kisses under her ear. She wanted to pull away but the feel of his gentle lips on her neck and the strong hold he had on her waist were undeniably intoxicating.

Kendall forced herself to snap out of her daze. "Daniel, what are you doing?"

"Not a lot, Princess, what about you?" he slurred. Kendall could smell the whisky the moment he opened his mouth.

He was absolutely hammered.

She swivelled round in his arms and saw his droopy, bloodshot eyes peering at her.

He was also high as a kite.

"Are you okay?" Kendall asked, concerned.

Daniel flashed a boyish grin. "Better now I'm with you, gorgeous."

There were those butterflies in her stomach again. Her skin felt hot where he held her and she was hyper aware of the quickening of her heartbeat.

"I think you should have some water," Kendall said, and attempted to hand him her bottle.

He looked down at it as if she'd asked him to drink vinegar.

He shook his head and moved closer, so she was pressed up against the fridge and he was towering over her, boxing her in with his arms. He placed a finger under her chin to force her to meet his gaze. He studied her intently, causing her lungs to feel as though they had lost every molecule of air. His face was so close that one more inch would have had them kissing.

Kendall wasn't sure if she wanted him to kiss her. She had never kissed anyone before and as attracted as she was to Daniel, she didn't want her first kiss to be with a drunk person who would never even remember it. She also wanted her first kiss to be with someone who was attracted to her at the very least, and she was certain that wasn't the case with Daniel.

"You're pretty," he slurred.

Flap

Flap

Those butterflies!

She cursed them silently for being so easily stirred.

It's not as if he meant it, she thought to herself.

She smiled sheepishly. "Thanks, Daniel."

She had heard those words many times before, but never believed them. She had heard that same compliment a million times, but had never internalised it, no matter how hard she tried.

"I love when you do that," he said.

"Do what?" she asked, puzzled.

He smirked. "I love it when you say my name." He paused drunkenly to take a breath. "And I love that you call me, Daniel, when no one else is allowed to."

She blushed and cast her eyes down to escape his burning gaze. She wanted to ask why no one else was allowed to call him by his name, but he spoke before she got the chance.

"I also love it when you get so nervous around me that you blush and look away."

Her face was on fire but she forced herself to meet his gaze and prove him wrong.

"I know it's because you're into me," he slurred.

Kendall froze and her eyes widened. She wasn't even sure why.

Was he even correct? she thought to herself.

"It's okay, Princess. I think you're hot too," he said, practically purring in her ear.

His eyes fluttered and he grinned lazily, continuing to study her face.

"Though I'm sure you already knew that," he added.

Yet another compliment that flew straight over her head.

His eyes darkened as he placed his hand on her hip, sliding it underneath the hoodie and onto her tight skirt.

Her skin went hot from his gentle touch.

She sent him a warning glare. "Daniel, you don't want me as your drunken hookup. There are plenty of better girls here that would oblige."

He frowned. "There is no one better. I want you and I want to be the only one who has you," Daniel slurred.

Kendall knew it was just the alcohol talking, but apparently the butterflies in her stomach didn't know it as they flapped their gigantic wings.

Confident now by her lack of response, Daniel moved his large hand from her hip to her ass, simultaneously moving his other hand there too.

Kendall knew there was no way Daniel would touch her like that if he was sober and she wasn't about to fall under his spell when he was completely wasted. He obviously didn't mean anything he was doing or saying.

"Daniel," she snapped, and his hands flew up in surrender.

She was ready to lecture him about getting some water and heading straight to bed, but before she could, he stumbled backwards and suddenly looked very dizzy.

Kendall knew he was on the verge of passing out, so she ran to look for Kai and Chris among the dancers, shouting that she needed help.

The three of them managed to get him up the enormous flight of stairs and into his room. Kai dragged Daniel into the bathroom and propped his head up on the toilet seat.

Kai promised to sort his friend out with the whole chundering situation and closed the bathroom door, leaving Chris and Kendall in the bedroom.

Kendall let out a sigh as the girls perched themselves on the end of the bed. Chris noticed her friend's wistful frown.

"What happened?" Chris asked.

Kendall faked a smile. "Nothing, I was just worried about him."

It didn't take X-ray vision to see right through Kendall's strong front.

"What did he say?" Chris asked, knowingly.

Kendall feigned confusion. "What do you-"

"Just tell me, babe," Chris cut her off.

Kendall sighed and gave in. "Just some flattering stuff that I know he didn't mean. He's hammered after all," she said, trying to brush it off casually.

Chris put her hand comfortingly on Kendall's shoulder. "Honey, drunk minds speak sober thoughts. Whatever he said, he meant it."

Kendall wanted to believe her. She wanted to think that everything Daniel said was true. But her mother's voice, as always, was there ready to shoot down any optimistic thoughts.

How could he ever think you're pretty?

You'll need to lose some weight before anyone is attracted to you.

He just wanted to get in your pants.

And not because he thinks you're hot, because you're easy and desperate.

Get real, honey... no one wants you.

Chris saw the wheels spinning in her friend's brain. She was trying to think of something that would prove her point. It bewildered Chris that someone so perfect and sweet could think so little of herself.

"Kendall, I'm going to tell you something and I'm not saying it for your benefit or mine. I'm saying it because it's true." She took a deep breath.

"I have known Dan for a while now and I have seen him win basketball games and hang out with his best friends. I've even seen him so high that he laughed so much it caused him to almost choke.

"But never in my life have I ever seen him happier than when he is with you.

"You may not have realised it but you are the first person who has never doubted him. When you tutored him, you were concerned that he would be irritating, but you weren't concerned that he was unteachable. He notices that look in teachers' eyes when they give up on him before they even try to teach him. He never saw that in you.

That means the world to him, though he would never admit it to you because of his pride.

"Not only that, but he is clearly territorial over you, which he never has been with other girls. He calls you a cute nickname and lets you call him by his actual name. That stuff may seem like nothing to you, but from someone who has known him a long time, I can confidently tell you that it means something.

"I am not saying he's in love with you and I can't guarantee what his true feelings are, but I can assure you that whatever he poured out to you downstairs was one hundred percent true. And it was only the tip of the iceberg," Chris finished firmly.

The bathroom door clicked open.

Chapter 15

Daniel and Kendall were alone in his room.

It had taken ten minutes for Daniel to persuade Chris and Kai to leave. He was still drunk but the vomiting seemed to have sobered him somewhat.

"Let's play a game," Daniel said.

Kendall chuckled. "Daniel, you need to go to sleep. You're going to be so hungover in the morning."

"The hangover won't be any the less for an extra thirty minutes of sleep, so come on," Daniel insisted. He was sprawled on his bed, leaning against the headboard.

She came to sit beside him, leaving a friendly distance.

She sighed. "Fine, what game?"

He smirked. "Twenty-one questions."

"That game is for thirteen-year-olds," Kendall said, unimpressed.

"I'm very in touch with my youth," Daniel said, leaving no room for argument.

Kendall huffed and leaned back on the headboard. "Fine. You go first."

"Why are you a cheerleader when you clearly don't like it?" he asked abruptly.

Her eyebrows rose.

She was at a loss, not having anticipated that he'd ask a question like that straight away.

"Um, I guess I kind of did it to fit in at first. But now I just don't know what I'd be without it. I would probably lose friends and cause drama and I just want this final year to go smoothly," she answered honestly.

He studied her face as he processed her response.

He was about to get her to expand on that, when she cut in. "Why be on a basketball team outside of school rather than joining the school team?"

He stared sleepily, clearly still feeling the effects of the alcohol. "I hate high school hierarchy."

She looked perplexed as she tried piecing together this response.

"Who was your first kiss?" he smirked.

She gulped, her cheeks flaming as she cast her eyes downwards in humiliation.

"Oh, um-" she stuttered, fiddling with the sleeve of his hoodie that she was still wearing.

"Wait," he interrupted, shocked.

"Don't tell me you've never-"

Her shamed face gave him the answer he was after.

He didn't seem to want to tease her for it; he just seemed utterly confused.

"How?" he said suddenly.

She shrugged.

"But how did you get those bruises if it wasn't from some guy you were seeing? You had a hickey." This new discovery had sobered him up almost completely.

Kendall chuckled and looked down. "I was never seeing a guy. My mother regularly tries to set me up with rich bachelors and she insisted this particular guy came to my room." She paused, swallowing her disgust, and she recounted the horrible event. "He never kissed me on the lips, but even if he had, I wouldn't count that as my first kiss."

Daniel was clenching the bed sheets so tightly his knuckles turned white. His jaw clenched as he stared into her wistful eyes, wondering how anyone could possibly want to hurt her.

She shook herself out of her pitiful daze and stood up.

"You should probably crash now. Congrats on your win today! I'll see you Monday," she said, walking backwards out of the door then scurrying down stairs and out the front door.

No way could she stay to hear Daniel's response. It scared her to think he might've said something to make her heart melt; something to make her feel warm and safe.

Maybe something that hinted at the possibility that someone might care for her?

Somebody who didn't just like her because of the people she was related to or associated with.

Someone who didn't see her as inferior to somebody else.

That scared her.

Chapter 16

For the first time in months, Kendall was in a good mood on a Monday.

'*What drugs did she take?*' one may ask.

Well, the answer is none. However, her mother had left for a two-week trip the night before, leaving her feeling lighter than ever.

She all but skipped over to her locker, struggling to hide her contentment. Ethan had started getting rides to school with the guy he had been flirting with at the party. Kendall didn't mind; he seemed to have quite the crush and she didn't want to stand in his way.

The weekend had also been a time for breakups as Austin and Megan had called it quits yet again.

Trouble in paradise for the tenth time that year. Queue the Kendall eye roll.

Regardless, she was in a great mood.

Until first period, where Daniel was a no show.

Against her better judgement she was excited at the thought of seeing him. She anticipated their time together with a great deal of enthusiasm.

She wasn't sure why. Or maybe she did know why, but didn't want to admit it to herself.

She decided to send him a quick text.

K: Hey are you coming in today? Should we reschedule the tutoring session?

A reply came through by the end of first period.

Big D: no and yes.

She quirked an eyebrow at the bluntness of the response but quickly dismissed it. She had to restrain a giggle at the username he had used in her phone.

***

That Monday had spawned another fiasco at lunch.

Megan looked ready to commit mass murder as she stomped to the cafeteria. Kendall knew she'd get all the details out from the sheep who wasted no time in jumping right into that can of worms.

Apparently, a new girl had arrived; small in height, average build, mousy brown hair, bland clothing, and big glasses. Her name was Daphne.

The problem was that Austin had been instructed to show her round and this had led to rumours that he'd been making moon eyes at Daphne all day.

Megan was livid.

All caught up on the drama, Kendall took her seat beside Ethan at their table. However, his attention was on Austin, who appeared to be staring fixedly on something across the cafeteria.

Or perhaps, *someone.*

Kendall followed his eye line to see a girl who matched the description of Daphne. But what the sheep had failed to mention was that she was absolutely beautiful.

Her big, blue almond eyes creased as she giggled at something the person across from her had said. She had full lips and round cheeks. Kendall could see no trace of makeup and she felt a pang of jealousy that someone could look so effortlessly pretty.

Despite Daphne's obvious beauty, Kendall knew that wasn't why Megan was so intimated.

It was the look in Austin's eyes. He appeared completely enamoured. Kendall felt inexplicably overjoyed.

Would it finally mean the end of the vicious cycle of Megan and Austin's toxic on-and-off relationship? she thought to herself.

***

Daniel didn't show on Tuesday either.

Kendall thought it odd that he was gone for two days in a row without so much as a text to tell her why.

Her insecurity made her think he was skipping school because he didn't want to see her, that he was embarrassed after what he had said when he was drunk.

'There is no one better. I want you and I want to be the only one who has you.'

Maybe he was worried she'd believed what he'd said, so he was staying away for a couple of days in case she got the wrong idea?

But logic told her he wouldn't even have remembered what he'd said. She sent him a quick text before she could talk herself out of it.

K: Are you ok?

No reply.

Maybe he *was* staying away from her.

***

Megan's jealousy was at an all-time high and arguably on the cusp of insanity.

"Find out everything about her; secrets, allergies, dating history, insecurities, EVERYTHING!" Megan barked furiously.

The sheep nodded obediently and frantically wrote down what she was saying on notepads or typed it into their apps.

Kendall felt she was the only sane person around.

She sighed. "Meg, don't you think this is all a bit drastic? She's only been here for a day and a half," Kendall reasoned.

Megan's eyes darted to her like an evil AI robot.

"No, this is not drastic. You haven't even seen drastic. She's put the target on her back, I'm just taking aim." She spoke harshly in a scarily calm voice. It was as though she didn't hear the craziness of her words.

Kendall rolled her eyes and walked away. Her patience was waning and Megan's screeching was a sure way of getting a splitting headache.

She made her way to the parking lot without paying attention to where she was going. Predictably her lack of concentration caused a collision and she sent herself and another girl tumbling to the ground.

Kendall groaned at the pain in her hip and looked up to see Daphne agitatedly gathering her scattered books and papers up from the floor. Kendall decided to help.

"I'm so sorry," Daphne squeaked, refusing to look at Kendall. The girl looked...

Petrified.

Kendall laughed softly. "No, I'm sorry. I wasn't looking where I was going." She handed the small girl the rest of her folders.

Daphne looked up at the sound of her voice and smiled gratefully. Her big blues softened.

"You're Daphne, right?" Kendall asked as they both stood up.

The girl looked alarmed at the sound of her own name.

"Yeah, how did you know that?" she asked, sceptically.

Kendall half-smiled sheepishly. "You're kind of the talk of the school, or at least the talk amongst my friends."

Daphne looked down nervously, something Kendall also did when she was embarrassed.

The girl gulped and met her gaze. "What's your name?"

"I'm Kendall, nice to meet you." She stretched her hand out and Daphne shook it.

"You too, Kendall. Sorry if I seemed kind of scared of you a second ago." She looked apologetic.

"Am I scary?" Kendall asked, giggling.

"Your whole friend group has been scaring me with dirty looks all day. Not you of course, but you're just intimidating by association and also because you're probably the most stunning person I have ever seen," Daphne said, rambling.

Kendall blushed at the compliment and refrained from looking down. "Thank you! That's really sweet."

They continued chatting for a further ten minutes or so before they parted ways.

Kendall found her to be warm and kind. She liked her. She wanted to be her friend.

Megan would not like that, she thought to herself.

***

Kendall's curiosity got the better of her on her way home and before she knew it, she was on Daniel Stryker's front porch.

She wanted to know why he was absent from school and ghosting her texts. His parent's cars weren't in the driveway so she assumed she wouldn't get him in trouble. *Hopefully.*

She knocked three times and there was a long pause before the door swung open.

Kendall gasped at the sight.

Chapter 17

Daniel stood before her in a black long sleeve top and black sweatpants.

This wasn't his usual lavish look but it wasn't that that made her heart skip a beat. It was the black eye and split lip, not to mention the torn-up knuckles.

He topped off the look with a scowl.

"What are you doing here?" he said, disgruntled.

"What happened to you?" Kendall asked, clearly concerned.

"I'm fine," he said dismissively.

Kendall laughed humourlessly. "Yeah, clearly."

"It's none of your business," he said flatly.

She looked at him in disbelief. "But it was your business when I had bruises on my wrists? You're such a hypocrite."

"What are you doing here?" he repeated.

She deadpanned. "You've been absent for two days and ignoring my texts. Naturally, I was worried."

"Okay, well I'm fine, so you can leave now." He dismissed her yet again and began to shut the door.

Her hand flew out to stop him. "How do you keep getting hurt so badly?" she asked.

"I'm fine. Leave," he demanded.

Kendall flinched. She knew she was poking a grizzly bear at this point so she'd have to pick her battles.

"I always get my way, Daniel. I will find out, whether you tell me or not," she finished confidently.

He quirked an eyebrow and suppressed an amused grin. "Is that a threat, *Princess?*"

Kendall smirked. "It's a promise."

She turned around and jumped into her car before he could utter another word.

***

Daniel was absent on Wednesday too.

Kendall wasn't surprised, he was in quite a state when she'd seen him the day before.

This could actually work in her favour in terms of finding out how he kept getting injured. It would be easier to dig around in his business if he wasn't there to stop her.

The horrifying thought that maybe his parents were abusive, had occurred to her. It would be stupid to disregard it as a possibility, but Kendall had a feeling there was something else going on. Perhaps it was insensitive to indulge her curiosity at the expense of Daniel's privacy, but seeing Daniel getting so badly hurt on a regular basis was not something she liked to witness.

Kendall marched into the school building and straight away sought out Kai and Blake.

After the usual polite greetings, she began her ambush.

"Why does Daniel have split knuckles and a bruised face yet again?" she blurted.

Kai's eyes widened in alarm while Blake remained cool as a cucumber and walked away.

Kai smiled sheepishly and nervously scratched the back of his neck.

"He is one clumsy little lad."

Kendall huffed and crossed her arms. "Please just tell me, or at least give me a clue."

"Um, Kendall... you know I can't tell you that if Daniel doesn't want you to know," he said.

Kendall pouted and tilted her head. "Please, Kai," she pleaded. "I'm worried about him."

Kai sighed and ran a hand through his hair. "I wish I could tell you but I can't. I'm sorry."

Well, that was a bust. She thought.

On to plan B.

***

Daniel, Kai and Blake had habitually smoked under the bleachers during second period everyday with two guys who don't attend high school. But now Daniel had stopped because he knew Kendall would castrate him for missing class, but she knew the others still did.

She asked to leave at the end of first period so that she could get to the bleachers before Kai and Blake. Luckily, she was a big hit amongst the teachers, so they pretty much let her do whatever she wanted.

She rounded the corner and sure enough Kai and Blake were nowhere to be seen, but one of the other guys was standing there, smoking. She held back a wicked grin as she mentally set her plan in motion.

"Hey, you," she said cheerily as she came to a halt in front of him.

He looked momentarily confused. "I haven't seen Daniel if that's who you're looking for."

Kendall smiled innocently and put on her girliest voice. "No silly, I was looking for you."

He visibly perked up. "Really? Why's that then, beautiful?" he said, making an attempt at a sexy voice.

Kendall cut straight to the chase. "Well, Daniel keeps getting injured, like someone is hurting him. But I don't think it's a one-way street because he also has split knuckles which leads me to believe he's also hurting someone else. He's clearly getting into fights regularly and I want to know why."

The guy seemed miffed that she wasn't actually there to see *him* personally but rather to ask about his friend.

"I take it you've already asked Kai and he gave nothing up, so what makes you think I will?" He straightened his posture in an attempt to look intimidating.

Kendall prepared herself for the performance of a lifetime.

She crossed her arms, pushing her breasts together to accentuate her cleavage. Just as she planned, his gaze darted to her chest and his eyes darkened with lust.

"I kind of thought that if you did me this favour by telling me what I want to know, maybe I could do you a favour," she said, looking up at him through her lashes.

His mouth was almost watering at her proposition.

"Come to a bar in town called 'Circuit' on Saturday night at 10pm and go downstairs. It costs fifteen dollars to get in," he said quickly, almost desperately.

Kendall grinned triumphantly and dropped her arms, backing away.

"Thanks!" She said over her shoulder and she turned to head to class.

"Hey, when're you gonna give me head?" he yelled.

Kai and Blake were suddenly there and had undoubtedly heard what he said.

Kendall blushed, but shaking off her embarrassment, she turned to face the guy who's name she still did not know. "I'm in high school you creep. Get a day job," she said, and stormed back inside.

***

The first football game of the season finally happened that Friday.

Kendall couldn't have cared less.

Daniel was back into school on Thursday and Friday, still looking battered. As soon as he saw her, he apologised for his previous rudeness and things quickly returned to normal between them.

Knowing she would learn more on Saturday night, Kendall was willing to bury that hatchet. Getting mad at him for not telling her seemed pointless.

She had even managed to convince him to attend her volleyball game on Sunday morning. She was glad he agreed because no one else would be there to cheer her on.

Her brother usually made it to all of her games and Ethan, too. But unfortunately, this Sunday there was a mandatory boot camp for any male who participated in sport at their school. She was disappointed they couldn't come, but she understood.

The cold September air brushed her bare legs as she finished the cheer routine and took her place by the stands to watch the remainder of the game.

Her school was winning by a landslide but Kendall wasn't really interested. She was happy that her brother was winning, but he always won, so it wasn't like it was anything to shout about.

As for cheerleading, she had lost interest in it by sophomore year when Megan became the official queen bee and instantaneously lost all substance to her personality. Megan was also captain, even though Kendall was a much better tumbler and a fair leader.

Kendall had accepted in junior year that talent and hard work do not necessarily always lead to success. Kendall knew she was a better cheerleader and would make a better captain, but Megan was idolised, so of course she was voted in. Again, Kendall ran for student body president with the highest GPA in school and an array of impressive extracurriculars, but Megan still won with nothing but cheer captaincy and a B- in English under her belt.

Kendall resented it but accepted it.

The only thing getting her through the game was the excitement of the following night when she would finally find out Daniel's secret.

She supposed she should probably feel bad for prying into his life and ambushing him with her arrival at an event she wasn't invited to, but she couldn't muster an ounce of remorse.

A chorus of loud cheers snapped her out of her thoughts and back into the muddy football field where Austin had just scored the winning touchdown.

Kendall clapped for him then braced herself for impact as the cheerleaders barged past her to leap into the arms of their favourite player.

Kendall was beyond pissed when she saw that the player Megan chose was Ethan. Megan wrapped her arms around Ethan's neck and kissed his cheek dramatically. Kendall felt her face flush with anger.

Austin witnessed the interaction but clearly thought nothing of it. He was looking into the stands and winking at someone. Kendall blinked away her rage and turned to see Daphne there, hiding her nervousness with an eye roll. Kendall smiled, genuinely happy to see this wholesome interaction.

An arm snaked around Kendall's waist and she turned to see the grinning face of Luke Cunningham. He was captain of the opposing team, the guy who'd had a fight with her brother the previous year. Luke had talked about nailing her right in-front of her brother. It had taken place when she'd showed up in the wrong size uniform and sent both teams into a frenzy. The memory of it embarrassed her to this day.

Luke was smirking confidently and keeping a firm grip on her waist.

"What are you doing, Luke? Get off me," Kendall snapped, trying and failing to pry his hand from her bare skin.

"Still feisty as ever, Ken. That's why I like you," he purred close to her ear, making her squirm.

"Hey jackass. Take a hike." Ethan materialised and suddenly Luke's body was torn from hers.

Kendall breathed a sigh of relief.

Luke flashed a cocky smile at Ethan, winked at Kendall and after looking her up and down, walked away.

Kendall looked at Ethan appreciatively. "Thank you."

"Of course." He smiled and pulled her into a hug.

"Ugh, you reek," she squeaked and pulled back.

"Megan didn't seem to mind," he said suggestively with an eyebrow wiggle. They began walking inside.

Kendall scrunched her nose in disgust. "Yeah, what was all that about?"

Ethan shrugged. "She was just trying to make Austin jealous. Kind of stupid to pick me though, Aussie trusts me enough to hang out with you without his supervision, so of course he trusts me not to get with Megan. Plus, he knows I can't stand her. She should've picked someone he's not as close with, they probably would've gone for it."

Kendall tilted her head sceptically. "Hm, I don't even know if that would've gotten to Austin. The first person he looked for in the crowd was Daphne. I honestly don't think he cares what Megan does anymore."

They continued chatting until they reached the boys' locker rooms. Kendall was heading home whilst everyone else went on to a celebratory party at Ethan's house. She had politely declined the invite.

She wanted to stay home and plan her outfit for the following night.

What does one wear when uncovering a scandal? she wondered.

Chapter 18

The taxi pulled up outside the bar and Kendall wasted no time in throwing ten dollars at the driver and launching herself out of the vehicle. She stared at the lit up sign that read 'CIRCUIT' and a shiver ran down her spine.

She handed the bouncer her fake ID, ignoring his disbelieving look. But he let her in anyway and she made for a staircase leading down to the basement. It was an older pub-style bar with a hideous red patterned carpet.

Kendall felt eyes sweeping her body as she skimmed the room. She was wearing black flares and a tight black waist coat. Her top showed more cleavage than she was normally comfortable with, but she wasn't sure what was appropriate and she wanted to look twenty-one.

She noticed an archway at the back end of the bar leading to a dark hallway. Booming music was coming from the bottom of the staircase, where a burly, unimpressed man was staring at her.

"How much to get in?" Kendall asked.

Without missing a beat, the man held out his hand. "Fifteen," he grunted.

She rummaged in her black Jacquemus Le Chiquito bag and handed him the money. He stepped aside and let her through.

The moment she entered the room she saw exactly what Daniel's secret was.

Swarms of people stood around drinking, looking expectantly towards the centre of the room, where there was...

A fighting ring.

Daniel was here, fighting illegally on Saturdays, and that's why he came in bruised and battered on Mondays. What was coming over the speakers confirmed her suspicions.

"UP NEXT, LADIES AND GENTLEMEN, WE HAVE THE REMATCH OF A LIFETIME."

The crowd erupted in cheers.

"WE HAVE BIG BRUCE COMING BACK FOR REDEMPTION AFTER GETTING ANNIHILATED TWO WEEKS AGO BY NONE OTHER THAN...

THE STRYKER!!"

The crowd roared and applauded as Big Bruce, a large muscular man, entered the ring, joined seconds later by Daniel.

Daniel wore loose red shorts with matching red boxing gloves. His expression was calm and stoic. There wasn't a trace of nerves, even though Big Bruce looked like a bodybuilder. Daniel was muscular and toned, like a Greek god, but Big Bruce looked like Dave Bautista.

Kendall spotted Kai, Blake, the two goons, and other miscellaneous people she assumed were Daniel's friends, at the ringside, shouting words of encouragement.

Daniel cracked his neck as the ref shouted out the basic rules and etiquette, but Kendall was too busy trying to slow her heart rate to hear anything.

His confident stance made it impossible for her to tear her eyes away from his glistening, flexed muscles under the dimmed lighting.

Without warning, the fight commenced and Kendall's heart dropped into her stomach. Daniel however, seemed unfazed as he circled his opponent.

Big Bruce delivered a hard punch but Daniel dodged it easily and delivered his own punch into Bruce's jaw, sending him stumbling back and clutching his face in obvious pain.

Kendall grimaced.

The fight continued pretty much on the same lines. Big Bruce kept trying to get Daniel with powerful blows but was too slow for Daniel's quick dodges. After approximately seven minutes of intense domination from Daniel, the fight was announced as finished and the crowd screamed with approval.

The crowd, including Daniel's friends, migrated upstairs to the bar to celebrate,

Kendall hid in the toilets for five minutes in order not to be seen by them. Eventually, she went upstairs and was surprised to see Daniel already in the bar, wearing grey sweatpants and a tight black T-shirt, and ordering a pint.

Kendall knew he would be pissed when he saw her there but for some reason, she still wanted him to see her.

She strolled up to the bar and stood beside him, but his back was to her as he chatted to his friends. Her arrival was a cue for silence to descend on the group.

"So, this is your dirty little secret, huh?" she said mischievously, causing him to swing around at the sound of her voice.

Yep... he looked pissed alright.

His elated expression from moments ago vanished. His dark blue eyes were burning a hole through her head.

"What the fuck are you doing here, Kendall?" he demanded through gritted teeth.

The use of her actual name rather than her usual nickname sent a cold shiver down her spine. He wasn't just pissed, he was *furious*.

Kendall smirked. "I told you I'd find out."

"Who told you?" he said quietly, each word dripping with anger.

Kendall made eye contact with the goon whose name she still didn't know. Everyone, including Daniel, turned to face him accusingly. The guy laughed nervously and hastily sipped his drink.

"What the hell, Skinner!" Daniel yelled.

Skinner was his name then, Kendall figured.

"She said she'd give me head," Skinner blurted desperately, as if it was going to help his case.

It didn't.

Kendall couldn't see Daniel's expression but she knew that had angered him further as he stood up straight, towering over a shaking Skinner.

"Bu- but she didn't!" Skinner stuttered.

Daniel visibly relaxed by around one percent upon hearing this and turned back to face Kendall.

"You need to leave right now," he said, trying to leave no room for argument.

Kendall scoffed. "No, I don't. I can hang around wherever I want, whether it bothers you or not."

Daniel stepped closer, his outraged face now close to hers.

She would be lying if she said she wasn't intimidated.

"Leave. I'm not going to ask you a third time," he commanded.

Kendall's face twisted in anger and defiance.

"No," she said.

Daniel chuckled humourlessly, then snaking an arm under her thighs, he threw her over his shoulder. She gasped at the sudden movement before fully registering that he was literally *throwing* her out.

He marched out of the bar, ignoring her demands to put her down, and threw her into the front seat of his car, strapping her in like a child.

And all the while she screamed at him to release her.

He hopped into the driver's side and locked the doors, so she was stuck. The engine revved and they were on their way to her house.

"Daniel let me out! You are way out of line. That was humiliating," Kendall said impatiently.

Daniel scoffed. "I'm way out of line? You pried into this part of my life after I specifically told you not to. What did you expect? That I'd be happy to see you?"

"Well, I certainly didn't expect to see you fighting illegally with people betting on you like you're a fucking pit bull," she said, lacing every word with venom.

He glared over at her and If looks could kill, she would have been six feet under.

"If you're waiting for an apology for dragging you out of there, then don't hold your breath. Someone like you shouldn't be in a place like that," he said.

Kendall looked at him in disbelief. "Someone like me? What does that even mean?"

"Someone who has her Daddy get her out of any minor inconvenience, who probably buys you a new pair of diamond earrings every time you're sad and comes to all of your volleyball games with a big poster of encouragement. You've definitely been sheltered from the real world for your whole life. You even said so yourself, you always get your way." He paused, running a hand through his hair. "They would eat you alive in there."

His words seared through her like a hot knife. His judgments and assumptions. She had kind of thought that as they'd got to know each other, they had become friends. She had definitely revised her opinion on him since first meeting him.

But his words had confirmed that he saw her as shallow, someone who didn't have to work for anything and if anything went wrong, daddy would be there to make it all better.

It couldn't be further from the truth, but Kendall wasn't about to tell him that.

They drove in a thick silence. When he pulled into her driveway she looked at him, pleadingly, then swallowed her pride.

"My volleyball game is tomorrow morning. Despite the events of this evening, I hope you still come. There won't be anyone else to cheer me on in the stands, so I'd really appreciate it if you were there," she said softly.

She hopped out of the car before he could respond.

She was mortified that she had just had to beg someone to come to her volleyball match.

She'd had to beg someone just to care about her.

Chapter 19

K endall tightened her ponytail and resumed her squatted position ready to take the shot.

Smack

She sent the ball hurtling towards the ground on the other side of the net, leaving no time for anyone to dive underneath it.

Another point.

Kendall felt encouraging pats on the back from her teammates as she scanned the stands.

Parents: absent of course. Brother: absent but with an adequate excuse. Ethan: absent but with an adequate excuse. Daniel: absent.

She sighed at the disappointing yet predictable turnout and got her head back in the game, shaking off the negativity.

The last point before the end of the second set was announced, and there would be a short break before the third and final set.

Once the game commenced, Kendall's teammate, Daisy, spiked the ball up in the air in Kendall's direction, setting up the perfect angle for Kendall to end the set in a single move.

The crowd roared as the ball hit the ground on the other side of the court yet again, without leaving any opportunity for the other team to save it.

The end of set two was announced and everyone headed over to grab water from the bench.

Daisy and Kendall high-fived and grabbed their bottles.

"Hey, Princess," someone whisper shouted.

Kendall looked up to see the one and only Daniel Stryker.

He wore a white long sleeve top over dark blue jeans and his usual devilish smirk. Kendall felt weak in the knees just from a single glance at him.

"I appreciate you coming but you're a little late, there's only one set left," Kendall said, re-tying her ponytail.

Daniel grinned and stepped forwards, attracting the attention of Kendall's teammates who were drooling at the sight of him.

"I've been here the whole time. I kind of hid myself amongst the crowd because I didn't want to throw you off with my incredibly irresistible good looks," he said with a smile.

Her heart skipped a beat.

"But now you're so far in the lead they can't overtake you, so I figured it was time to come out of the shadows," he finished.

Kendall blushed at his thoughtfulness and looked down nervously at her water bottle.

"You're killing it out there. I knew you'd be good but damn, you could go pro," he said assuredly.

Before Kendall could dispute this assertion, the speakers announced the beginning of the final set.

Daniel smiled encouragingly and she backed away and took her position on the court.

The red-headed girl across from her on the other team flashed her a cocky smile. "You're seeing Dan Stryker?" she said almost mockingly.

"None of your business," Kendall spat, her expression giving nothing away.

The girl smirked. "So, you're his new flavour of the month? Enjoy it while it lasts, *Babe*. He'll make you the happiest you have ever been for a few seconds, then he'll treat you like a stranger. Just thought you should know," she added, smiling innocently

Kendall's blood boiled. It didn't take a genius to know she was trying to psyche her out. But it couldn't be a coincidence that the girl knew Daniel's name and his reputation. She had basically confirmed that the two of them had slept together.

And that bothered Kendall.

The game began and Daisy sent the same move that had finished the second set. As the ball came towards Kendall her rage took over. She hit the ball with an obscene amount of aggression and sent the ball straight into the red headed girl's face.

The girl tumbled backwards, clutching her nose with a painful grunt. Blood poured down the lower half of her face and the whistle was blown for a timeout.

Kendall's expression remained dark with no trace of remorse. The girl with the bloody nose stared coldly up at her, filling Kendall with a warm and fuzzy satisfaction.

That nice feeling dissipated though, when her coach yelled her name in fury and benched her for the remainder of the game.

Kendall took her seat. Her team, many of whom were holding back laughter, had already won; she wouldn't have made such a rash decision if this had not been the case.

The injured girl was rushed to the medical room and the game resumed. Kendall quickly got bored with watching without being able to jump in, so she told her coach she needed the bathroom and left the gym.

She stood in the hallway outside the changing rooms and sighed.

At the sound of footsteps, she turned to see Daniel walking towards her.

"That was quite the show. Not that I didn't enjoy it but what did that poor girl do to deserve such an obviously deliberate attack?" he asked, amused as he leaned against the wall.

"You didn't recognise her? That steamy night you had must only have been memorable for her then," she challenged

Seemingly confused, he looked up and pondered.

Then realisation struck him. "Ohh, right yeah," he said casually, meeting her gaze.

Kendall turned hot with anger. She couldn't pinpoint why, it's not as if it had been recent, considering he barely recognised her. And even if it was recent, why should it bother Kendall?

He smirked and leaned in closer. "You broke a girl's nose because she told you we hooked up?" he said in cocky disbelief.

Kendall looked down, embarrassed and muttered, "No."

Daniel's chest vibrated with laughter.

"You know, Princess, if I didn't know any better, I'd say you're *jealous*," he said smugly.

Kendall looked up at him and scoffed dramatically.

"As if, Daniel," she said. But he didn't seem convinced by her denial.

He took a step forward, so there was virtually no space between them.

Her breath hitched in her throat.

He continued staring at her flustered state, loving the effect his close proximity had on her.

"Are we just going to pretend last night didn't happen?" Kendall demanded.

Daniel's confidence waned and his smirk fell away.

"Are we just going to pretend that it's not completely outrageous that nobody else came to support you today? Where's your family?" he countered.

Kendall fake gasped and put her hand on her heart dramatically. "You mean that insulting assumption you made about my family adoring me and sheltering me from everything has actually turned out to be false?!" She paused to regain a serious demeanour. "Yes, nobody showed up because my brother is busy and my mother couldn't care less. She doesn't even know I play volleyball, much less that I'm captain."

Daniel looked like a kid being yelled at.

"I'm sorry, I shouldn't have said that. I didn't mean it, I was just mad," he said.

Kendall nodded to indicate he was forgiven.

"What about your dad? If you don't mind me asking," Daniel said.

She looked down to hide her distaste at the mention of her father.

"He left a while back," she answered briefly and without emotion.

Daniel's face dropped. It clearly wasn't the answer he was expecting.

"Now can we talk about last night?" Kendall asked, raising an eyebrow.

Daniel huffed and ran a hand through his soft dark hair. "Fine. What do you want to know?"

"How long have you been doing it?"

"Three years," he said without hesitation.

"Do you fight every week?" Kendall asked.

"Mostly, yes."

"Do you get money?"

"Yes, a lot."

"Have you ever lost?"

"Not once," he said confidently.

Kendall studied his stoic face. "Why do you do it? It's not like you are short on cash."

"I like winning," he said simply.

Kendall quirked an eyebrow at the lacklustre response, urging him to elaborate.

He sighed.

"My siblings are both more than 12 years older than me. I was the accident child my parents didn't want because they already had two perfect children. My brother succeeded massively in sports and my sister succeeded academically. I spent my whole life trying to prove I was just as good as my brother and sister. It was exhausting and virtually impossible, since they had already done everything first. Impressing my parents was so hard it made me angry. I got into fighting to deal with the rage and experience success in my own right without the pressure of my parents' watching eyes. I like basketball so I continue to play it but I don't tell my dad about my wins because he will just use it as a way to compare me to my brother or even himself. No one in my family has won every week at fighting. It gives me something that's mine. I'm good at it, too. It also gives me financial independence which helps hugely in my house.

"I guess I just like the glory. It's a nice change from being in the shadow of other people all the time," he finished.

Kendall stared, fascinated. Now she was really looking, she could see the pain behind his eyes. She saw the neglect and the protective barriers he erected to protect from further pain.

She knew how that felt.

"That makes sense," she said, reassuringly.

"So, you don't think I'm a bad guy now, right? Just because I punch people?" he asked, optimistically.

Kendall giggled. "I don't think you're a bad guy, Daniel."

He smiled down at her.

She had no idea how much those words meant to him, especially coming from her.

"But just so you know, you are never coming to another fight," he added.

She scowled. "What! Why?!"

"Because all kinds of people go to those fights, especially the kind of men who would see a beautiful woman like you and want to have you."

Kendall's heart skipped a beat at the word, 'beautiful'. It wasn't as if she hadn't been called that before, but when Daniel said it, it felt like she was hearing it for the first time.

"Well, can you blame them?" Kendall joked.

Daniel deadpanned. "I'm serious. You're not safe there."

Kendall huffed. "You're not the boss of me. I think we have already discovered that I don't take no for an answer, so sorry Daniel, but I will be there."

"Fine. As long as you're okay with being carried out of there again like last night," he said with a smug grin.

"Hey! I wasn't ready for that but from now on, it won't be so easy. I can be very scrappy you know," Kendall argued.

Daniel bit his lip in an effort to hold back laughter at her adorable attempt to intimidate him.

"Yeah. okay, Princess," he said condescendingly.

"Have we forgotten that I broke a girl's nose a mere ten minutes ago?" Kendall said.

Daniel smirked and took a step closer. Their chests were touching, their faces an inch apart, and his arms were up against the wall behind her, caging her in.

"Oh, I haven't forgotten, Princess," he purred.

She gulped.

He moved his mouth over to her ear and whispered, "In fact, it was pretty hot watching you get all territorial over me."

Shivers ran through her from her ear down to her toes and her breathing became uneven.

"You have such a hold on me, Princess," he said softly, into her neck.

He brought his face back to hers, only a centimetre apart, and her brown eyes bored into his.

He watched as she bit her lip nervously, prompting him to wet his lips with his tongue. She looked at his plump wet lips, so inviting.

He noticed her staring and smirked.

He knew what he wanted to do and he was almost completely certain she wanted it too.

Without warning, he crashed his lips onto hers.

Chapter 20

S uddenly the world went quiet.

His lips were soft and slow, allowing her to keep up after having the breath completely knocked out of her.

He sucked on her bottom lip gently and they both tilted their heads to allow the kiss to deepen. His left hand went to her lower back to pull her body impossibly close to his, whilst his right thumb gently caressed her jaw.

His tongue swiped her lip and a faint noise of satisfaction escaped the back of her throat. She felt him smirk against her lips.

The wolf whistles startled them both and they broke the kiss, turning to look down the hall at the intrusion.

Her volleyball team stood awestruck, clearly having seen what was about to become a heavy make out session. Kendall turned redder than the blood that had poured out of the nose she'd broken earlier and she removed herself from Daniel's hold.

The girls smiled approvingly and wiggled their eyebrows as they walked past, giggling on their way to the locker room.

Daniel chuckled and scratched the back of his neck. Kendall gave a tight smile.

"Well, see you in school," she chirped and made a break for it towards the locker room.

"Wait." He gently grabbed her arm.

She turned slowly.

"You're not gonna be super awkward around me now, right? No avoiding me?" he said amused and fighting a grin at her flustered state.

"Of course not!" she squeaked and pelted through the door to safety.

Or what she thought was safety.

Her team descended like vultures to hear what had happened. Kendall kept it vague and changed the subject back to the game as soon as she could.

She wasn't even sure she could explain what happened, even if she tried.

Kendall wasn't sure herself what had happened.

'You have such a hold on me, Princess.'

***

Kendall realised she could not possibly live up to their agreement about not being awkward around Daniel.

He sat next to her in physics and in the silence that ensued she could hear her pulse thumping in her ears.

He seemed amused by the effect he had on her and she was relieved he wasn't annoyed that she was doing exactly what she'd said she wouldn't do.

She just needed time to get used to being around him again, and something told her he knew that.

He didn't seem to mind that she didn't speak the entire morning. In fact, he had become such a good student over the few weeks she'd been helping him, that it was now normal for him to pay attention to the teacher and get on with the work when it was assigned.

And he did exactly that.

Lunchtime brought the usual drama. However, Kendall was the one providing it this Monday afternoon.

She had realised she could not continue to stay on the cheer team just to appease Megan. She was at the end of her tether and she was no longer afraid of Megan's reaction.

Megan's jaw was inches from the floor when Kendall broke the news. Her eyebrows shifted south and her fists balled.

"Excuse me? You can't quit. Why would you even want to quit?" Megan said squeakily.

Kendall grimaced at the screechy tone.

"You can't change my mind. I haven't been enjoying it for a long time and I've wanted to quit for ages, but I didn't want to upset you," Kendall said firmly.

Megan rolled her eyes and stabbed at her cob salad with a fork. "Whatever, Kendall, it's not like you even show up to practice any-more, anyway."

"I was injured," Kendall said defensively.

"Don't lie, Kenny. It's fine if you haven't been enjoying it but you could've told me the truth earlier," Megan patronised.

Kendall nodded silently.

Megan plastered on an innocent smile. "I just hope you know what you're giving up. I mean, do you really think guys will be interested in you once you stop shaking your ass in a mini skirt at every football game?"

The table fell silent.

Luckily, it was just girls there, otherwise Kendall's embarrassment would be up to the level of fleeing the cafeteria.

"But I guess you don't really care about any other guys' attention now that you're hooking up with that lowlife," Megan spat.

Kendall's face was so hot she was sure she'd burn herself if she touched it. She knew Megan was referring to Daniel. Her palms were sweating and her jaw was clenched to the point where it was painful. She was furious at the disrespect towards Daniel and the insinuation that she was sleeping with him.

Before she could blow-up on Megan, one of the sheep chimed in.

"You're with Dan?! You're so lucky, he's so hot," the sheep gushed, causing the other sheep to nod and giggle.

"Shut up!" Megan hissed, silencing the table.

"For your information, he's not a lowlife. He's actually a pretty incredible basketball player and he's very intelligent. Regardless, I'm not sleeping with him." Kendall said with deadly eye contact in Megan's direction.

Megan giggled mockingly. "You're right. What was I thinking? He wouldn't sleep with *you*."

Kendall slammed her tray against the table and stood up. "I have so much dirt on you, Megan. You want to belittle me? I could make you so embarrassed you'd stay home from school for a month."

Megan's smirk dropped and the sheep exchanged nervous looks.

"Come to me when you want to apologise," Kendall said calmly, and headed straight to class.

***

The final two classes of the day went by without incident.

Kendall still wasn't feeling comfortable enough to speak to Daniel and her argument with Megan didn't exactly increase her confidence.

Daniel didn't seem to mind. She'd caught him smirking at her a couple of times whilst she frantically wrote notes or answered questions.

She pretended not to notice.

After fifth period Kendall told Daniel she'd meet him in the library for tutoring, and headed to her locker.

Unfortunately, Megan and her sheep were surrounding it. Kendall huffed but continued her quest anyway.

Megan turned to her with the fakest pout the world had ever seen.

"I'm sorry, Kenny. I hate it when we fight," she said in a babyish voice.

Kendall resisted the urge to roll her eyes and instead faked a smile. She opened her locker and gathered her things for the tutoring session with Daniel.

"So, when do we need the wasps for, Meg?" One of the sheep said.

Kendall choked on air.

Megan aggressively patted her back until the coughing subsided.

"Wasps?" Kendall said exasperated.

Megan gasped with excitement. "OH-EM-GEE!! We totally forgot to tell Kenny about the plan!"

Kendall felt like plugging her ears as Megan squealed at a frequency only dogs could hear.

The sheep spoke up to explain. "Okay, so Megan had this brilliant idea to put wasps in Daphne's locker after we'd done some digging and found out she's allergic!"

The sheep looked at her, excitedly, like it was the best game plan since Operation Barbarossa.

Kendall's face showed her concern. "You can't be serious?"

"Of course she's serious! How else are we gonna teach that bitch who's boss?" Megan said.

Kendall looked dumbfounded. "Megan, this isn't some silly prank that will make her run into the bathroom crying. If she doesn't carry an EpiPen on her she could go into anaphylactic shock!"

Megan looked unfazed and the sheep looked like this was brand new information to them.

Megan scoffed dismissively, "You don't know that."

"That's the thing! We don't know exactly what could happen because we don't know how allergic she is! But wasp and bee stings are known to send allergic people into anaphylactic shock if they aren't treated with an EpiPen immediately and anaphylactic shock can kill people." Kendall yelled.

"What is with you?!" Megan hissed.

Kendall's eyes widened. "What's with me?! What the hell is with you?!

"You're so obsessed with my brother that you're putting a girl's life on the line. That is *psychotic*!" Kendall said wildly.

Megan's expression grew bitter and she took an intimidating step towards Kendall.

"If you don't like how I do things... then you can leave. As far as I'm concerned, you've been dead to this group for a while now. But just so you're aware, if you're not with us, you are against us," Megan said, venom lacing every word.

Kendall's death glare didn't falter and she didn't move a muscle.

"You can even join Daphne as target number one. It makes it easier since I already know all of your weak spots," Megan taunted.

"Go ahead," Kendall smirked, "I can take it. Besides, it'll be funny when Austin and Ethan completely shun you along with the rest of the guys because they will side with Austin."

Megan looked like steam could pour from her ears.

"See ya." Kendall chirped and bumped Megan's shoulder as she walked past.

Chapter 21

D aniel clicked and unclicked his pen for the hundredth time. He sighed impatiently as he sat watching the library door, waiting for her to walk in all nervous and awkward. But when the door finally swung open and Kendall walked in, she wasn't nervous or awkward at all, she was raging.

She stomped over to the table and slamming her books down, she ran a frustrated hand through her hair then sank down into her seat.

He couldn't hide his smirk.

She met his gaze and scowled at his amused expression. "I'm sorry, is my misery amusing to you?"

He chuckled, causing her to frown.

"I was just wondering whether you knocked out another girl I've been with? You are the jealous type after all," Daniel said teasingly.

"I am not!" she blurted.

He laughed again and leaned forwards, bringing his face closer to hers and said in a lowered voice, "Don't worry, Princess, I already told you I don't mind."

The blush she'd been suppressing all day spread across her cheeks and she began arranging her books to seem busy.

He stared at her flustered state, amused. He knew exactly what to do and say to induce this reaction.

"Ok, why are you actually mad?" he asked genuinely, dropping the smirk, "And late?"

She looked at him guiltily, "I'm sorry I was late. I got into a huge argument with Megan and basically ended our friendship and now I'm number one on her hit-list."

He quirked an eyebrow. "Wow. That all happened pretty quickly, you were only ten minutes late."

She giggled, feeling the tension from the argument lessen. "Yeah, I guess it did all happen pretty fast."

"What was it about?" he asked.

Kendall sighed.

"Megan is not a big fan of the new girl, Daphne. She's been getting so much of Austin's attention, leaving Megan with none. Megan came up with this psychotic plan to put wasps in Daphne's locker because she's allergic. I explained how dangerous and insane that plan was and Megan didn't like that."

Daniel looked dumbfounded. "You're right, that is psychotic."

"Yeah," Kendall laughed.

"You might want to warn Daphne to have her EpiPen on standby whenever she's at school," Daniel suggested.

"Yeah, I think I might," Kendall said.

Daniel looked at her with a boyish grin.

"What?" she said, confused.

"You stopped being all awkward and weird around me. I knew you'd come around," he said smiling.

Kendall laughed nervously and looked down at her books, blushing yet again.

"I guess I did," she said sheepishly.

Daniel couldn't help but stare at her. He loved the effect he had on her and he loved even more that she tried to hide it. He found it fascinating just watching her, it was as if he could see the wheels turning in her brain just by looking into her dark eyes.

An idea suddenly struck her and her face lit up like a light bulb. "Oh! There's a party this Friday at some footballer's house. You should come."

He smiled.

"Are you asking me out?" he asked with raised eyebrows.

She rolled her eyes. "Well, the party is technically out, because it is outside of your house and I'm asking if you want to come, because otherwise I'll be dreadfully bored by myself."

Daniel chuckled at her attempt to spell out exactly what she meant, to ensure there was no confusion.

"Sure, Princess. Just don't forget the wedding's the next day, so let's not go crazy with the shots."

Her eyes widened and her jaw dropped.

"That's this weekend?!" she blurted.

Daniel furrowed his eyebrows in confusion, "Yeah, I thought you knew that?"

"No! I clearly did not know that. I need to get a dress and we need to do some more studying about each other," she said frantically.

"Oh, I'll happily do some studying on you, Princess," he said, looking her up and down suggestively.

She scowled and kicked his leg under the table. "I'm serious."

He groaned and rubbed his shin. "Okay, Okay. Let's get started then."

***

Kendall returned home that afternoon feeling a weight lifted from her shoulders. She was finally free from the wicked witch of the west and she and Daniel were more than prepared for questions about their knowledge of each other. Daniel had agreed to come to the party on Friday, and he had agreed to go dress shopping with her on Thursday to pick something his family would approve of. On top of that, he had offered her a place at his and his friends' lunch table, now that she, in his words, was 'a loner'.

And if all of that wasn't great enough, her mother was away until the Monday of the following week.

She threw herself on the couch like a starfish and wrapped a blanket around her, snuggling into the shape of a ball. Then she turned on the tv to watch reruns of Boy Meets World.

Four episodes later, the front door opened and Austin walked in. He was sweaty and dirty, clearly having just finished practice.

"Hey, little one!" he yelled in greeting.

He dumped his gear on the floor and joined her on the couch, perching on the small space on the very end that was all that was available thanks to her long, sprawling limbs.

"Hey," she replied half-heartedly, still focused on the TV.

Austin took the remote and paused the program. Kendall gave him a murderous glare. As he snatched the blanket off of her and threw it behind the couch, she sat up and went to slap his arm. Trying not to laugh, he grabbed both of her hands.

"What the hell!" she yelled.

"I want to talk to you and I need your full attention," he said, releasing her wrists and leaning back into the couch.

She huffed but gave in none-the-less. "Fine, hurry up."

"I heard what happened with you and Megan today," he said.

Kendall quirked an eyebrow. "From who?"

"Greg heard you guys, he hid behind the corner and heard it all," Austin said casually.

"That's invasive, but whatever," Kendall said.

Austin chuckled and looked at her comfortingly. "Are you okay?"

Kendall shrugged. "Not looking forward to whatever brutal things she's planning for my demise, but I was over being her friend ages ago and I meant everything I said."

"You're a brave person for standing up to her, she's got a lot of ways to make your life hell," Austin said sympathetically.

"She doesn't scare me."

Austin smiled genuinely. "Good. You know Ethan and I have got your back."

Kendall nodded.

"And for what it's worth, thanks for sticking up for Daphne. Megan is clearly more insane than I thought. I underestimated her," Austin said, looking down nervously when he mentioned Daphne.

"Of course, she doesn't deserve Megan's wrath. I like her. I can tell you do, too." Kendall smirked.

Austin scratched the back of his neck. "Is it that obvious?"

"Yes."

Her lack of hesitation made Austin chuckle.

He looked at Kendall accusingly. "Well, what about you and Daniel? I've never seen you so smitten."

Kendall sighed. "Aussie, don't-"

"I'm not gonna get all protective on you right now," he cut her off.

"I actually like him. He seems to make you happy and he hasn't given me any reason to beat him up," he continued.

The corners of Kendall's mouth twitched into a smile.

"Besides, I heard he came to cheer you on at your volleyball game at the weekend when I couldn't. He must care about you," Austin finished, with the ghost of a smile.

Kendall jumped into his arms and her brother embraced her, chuckling softly.

Chapter 22

The following day, Daniel was sitting with Kai and Blake at lunch, waiting for Kendall to make an appearance.

Kai had been staring at Daniel suggestively for five minutes while Daniel, pretending not to notice, wolfed down his burger.

"So, she's eating lunch with us now?" Kai said giddily.

Daniel deadpanned, "So?"

"You like her."

Daniel rolled his eyes and turned back to his burger.

Kai took this as an invitation to continue, knowing exactly what to say to get Daniel to admit it.

"If you aren't keeping her around because you like her, then when're you gonna tap that? Because if you don't, I will," Kai said confidently.

There was a pause before Daniel huffed agitatedly and shot Kai a warning glare.

"Talk about her like that again and see what happens," Daniel spat.

Kai smirked and Blake chuckled beside him.

"So... is that because you don't like her?" Kai teased.

Daniel grunted and was about to rip Kai a new one but was interrupted by a female presence behind him.

"Hey guys," Kendall's angelic voice relaxed his entire body.

The boys greeted her and she took a seat and placed her salad on the table.

She poked at her salad and quickly got into discussion with Blake about 'Keeping Up with The Kardashians' as they had recently discovered a mutual interest in reality TV. Daniel gazed at her smilingly.

Kai noticed the longing gaze and waggled his eyebrows at his delusional friend. Daniel threw a fry at him. To his dismay, Kai caught it in his mouth and smirked triumphantly.

***

Daniel used every ounce of self-restraint not to take his right hand off of the steering wheel to punch Kai straight between the eyes.

"I don't get why you won't admit that you *love* her," Kai taunted, elongating the word 'love' for extra emphasis.

Blake cut in, "Kai, just quit it already. Can we collect Christina on the way please?"

Daniel huffed in relief. "Yeah, Kai, do as you're told. And yes, I will get Chris."

Kai crossed his arms and shook his head in denial.

Daniel pulled up to the side of the road where Chris was waiting outside her apartment complex. She hopped into the back and leaned into Blake's side.

"Hello, ugly people," she greeted them, then leaned forward to speak to Daniel. "Hey Stryker, did you see your Mija today?"

Daniel rolled his eyes and snorted.

"I have an eject button and I'm not afraid to use it," he warned.

Chris smirked and leaned back into Blake's embrace.

"He won't admit he likes her, even though I caught him staring at her at lunch with love-heart eyes," Kai blurted.

Chris and Blake chuckled and Daniel flipped them the middle finger from the front seat.

Chris suppressed her laughter. "Danny, if it's any consolation, I'm almost certain she likes you too."

"What makes you say that? Did she tell you?" he said, trying to sound cool and uninterested.

Chris giggled at the sudden change in his voice. "I'm not telling you what we talk about, but speaking as a third-party observer, it seems kind of obvious."

Daniel smirked smugly.

"I mean, do you know how many guys show an interest in her? They're like moths to a flame. And she's a pretty hot flame, let's not lie," Chris said dramatically.

Daniel squeezed his eyes shut momentarily in frustration. "I don't need to be reminded of how many guys want her, I figured that out for myself."

"Aw, don't be jealous, Danny boy. She clearly only reciprocates in your case," Chris said reassuringly, whilst Kai patted his shoulder.

Daniel silently hoped Chris was right.

***

Kendall fiddled nervously with her sleeve as she stood in the school locker room waiting to head into the sports hall to try out for the school's volleyball team.

She figured it made sense now that she was off of the cheerleading team and had some extra time. It would mean double the practice, because she had no intention of dropping out of her team outside of school. She would be on two teams.

The girls greeted her warmly and introduced her to the team.

The atmosphere here was so different from the cheerleading squad.

An hour later the try outs were over and unsurprisingly, she had made the team. Despite her obvious ability, she was still thrilled to have made the team. The girls were all genuinely nice, in huge contrast to the cheer squad.

Once back in the locker room Kendall took her time having a shower and blow drying her hair. There was no rush since school was over, so she wrapped herself in a fluffy white towel and put on some casual make-up. Now she was ready to meet Daniel, as agreed, in the library for their tutoring session.

However, she was shocked to her very core when she opened her gym locker and found all her clothes gone! Not even her volleyball kit was there. She knew immediately who was behind it.

Megan.

She turned towards the other girls, feeling awkward. "Guys, someone has stolen all my clothes."

They gasped and looked at her as if she'd grown two heads.

"That's crazy," one of the girls said.

"Who do you think could have done it?" said another.

Kendall chuckled, "Oh, I know who it was."

They looked at her expectantly, waiting for her to blurt out the name of the culprit.

"Does anyone have any clothes? I know it's a long shot but I need something to wear so I can go and get mine back?" Kendall asked.

The girls looked at one another guiltily, confirming it was a no.

Kendall nodded in understanding and turned back to her locker. "*Fuck you, Saunders,*" she muttered under her breath.

Chapter 23

K endall stared at her locker for a good five minutes, hoping a solution would hit her if she stood still long enough.

Megan had left only her shoes, socks, and her phone.

Kendall considered calling someone but she wasn't sure there was anything anyone could do.

The girls all apologised for not being able to help and offered to stay with her until she figured something out, but Kendall told them it was fine.

She was alone in the locker room, perched on a bench wearing nothing but a towel.

She sighed and swallowing her pride, texted Daniel.

K: I need your help!

Big D: Gonna need you to be a bit more specific, Princess :)

K: Megan stole my clothes.

K: All I have are shoes, socks and a towel.

Big D: Well, she wasted no time kicking you in the teeth then

ig.

K: Please tell me you can help.

Big D: I have some clothes in the back of my car. I'll be 10 minutes. Where are u?

K: Oh, just lying in the middle of the hallway.

Big D: Ha, ha. You're so funny.

K: I'm still in the locker room, obviously.

Big D: No need for the attitude.

K: Hurry up, dumbass.

Ten minutes later there was a knock on the door.

"Daniel?" she asked, just in case.

"Can I come in?" came Daniel's voice from outside.

Kendall opened the door slightly to be greeted by Daniel's handsome face. Relieved, she opened the door wide and let him in.

He was smirking, eyeing her towel-clad body. Kendall blushed uncontrollably and suddenly felt she wanted another shower.

"Looking good, Princess," he said smugly.

Kendall stomped over to the bench and sat down, making sure to cross her legs. "Shut up."

He took a seat beside her and placed his clothes in her lap. "Be nice. I'm here saving your naked ass," he said, with an amused smirk and trying not to laugh.

She looked down at the clothes to see what she was working with. It was a black hoodie and black sweatpants.

"I keep spare clothes in my car for after fights and stuff," he said casually.

"Thanks," she said, smiling slightly as she looked into those dark blue eyes that always took her breath away.

"I'll change in the showers," she said, standing up.

"That's okay, I don't mind you changing here," Daniel said cheekily.

Kendall rolled her eyes at his smirk.

"I'm sure you wouldn't mind, especially since my underwear was also stolen," Kendall said before she could stop herself.

Realising she'd spoken out loud her eyes widened in alarm. She heard Daniel chuckling behind her and she squeezed her eyes shut.

"So, you're going commando in my clothes? That's actually pretty hot."

Kendall heard the smirk in his voice. Refusing to turn round she went straight into the showers and changed.

The hoodie drowned her in the most comfortable and cosy way possible. The sweatpants were far too big so she pulled the drawstrings as tight as they could go. They *had* to stay up, considering she was completely bare underneath.

She put her shoes and socks on, sitting beside Daniel on the bench.

"I like you in my clothes," he said.

"I'd be happier with something on underneath, but this is pretty comfortable. Thanks for rescuing me," Kendall said, smiling.

Outside the locker room, Kendall was set to find Megan and curse her out. Storming through the hallways, with an amused Daniel in tow, she shoved open the exit doors and scanned the parking lot for a giggling mop of blonde hair.

Megan and the sheep were there, standing near a car, with a few basketball players dotted in between them. Kendall made her way over.

Megan put on a sickly-sweet smile when she noticed Kendall's arrival and the sheep shut up. But before she could even open her mouth to snap at the evil blonde, something on the floor caught her eye.

A pile of sopping wet clothes lay on the concrete. *Her clothes.*

"Figured your clothes probably needed a wash now that you're hanging out with trash," Megan said, a smug grin plastered across her face.

Kendall's blood boiled at the insult; Daniel was very much within earshot. She turned to see if Daniel would retaliate, but he looked completely unbothered and just stood there with his arms crossed.

"You guys took a little while in the locker rooms. Oh, and now you're in his clothes! Did you have a quickie in the showers?" Megan tilted her head tauntingly as she spoke.

"Do you seriously have nothing better to do? What a pitiful existence you lead, Megan," Kendall said calmly.

She swore she heard Daniel chuckle behind her.

Megan put her hand on her heart and pouted. "Aw, that might actually hurt if I cared even slightly about your opinion."

"What do you even want? Each one of your tortuous games just proves even more that you're threatened by me," Kendall said.

Megan's smirk dropped; it was clear Kendall had struck a nerve. Megan stepped forward as if to raise her hand at Kendall, but the captain of the basketball team, who was draped across Megan, put his arm out and stopped her

Kendall smiled. "Don't make this a physical fight, you know you'll lose that one."

Megan and the sheep gave her a mean-girl-up-and-down look.

Kendall turned to see Daniel's lopsided grin. The two of them headed over to where Kendall's car was parked.

Daniel leaned against the side of the Ferrari and crossed his arms. "You handled that pretty well."

Kendall shrugged, "I'm very used to her stupid little games. Sorry she came after you too, although you didn't seem fazed."

Daniel chuckled, "She doesn't bother me, especially as her friends were drooling over me the entire time."

Kendall deadpanned, "No they weren't."

"I'm being so serious," Daniel insisted.

Kendall laughed and shoved his arm playfully.

"Our tutoring session kind of got put on hold, didn't it," Daniel said.

"Yeah, sorry about that. Come back to my house and we can have it there. My parents are out of town," Kendall said casually.

Daniel raised his eyebrows and smirked cheekily.

Kendall realised what she had implied by mentioning her parents weren't home and began frantically to try to explain herself. Daniel just laughed at her.

They got into their cars and headed to Kendall's house.

Chapter 24

Kendall swung her bedroom door open and plopped onto the bed. Daniel followed her in and immediately began snooping around, picking up trophies and picture frames, zooming in with his eyes. The one thing he put down instantly as if it had burnt him, Kendall noted, was a picture of her and Ethan.

"Cute room," he said, eyeing it up.

He began opening drawers at random. Kendall didn't think anything of it until she saw a black laced thong dangling from his finger.

"Who's the black lace for, Princess?" he smirked.

She leapt off of the bed and went to snatch the underwear out of his hand but he held it up high, out of her reach.

Kendall gave him her bored look. "Are you really gonna make me jump?"

He raised a challenging eyebrow.

She rolled her eyes and jumped, snatching it out of his hands with ease. Daniel looked impressed.

"Bravo. I guess volleyball is helpful in day-to-day life," he said.

Kendall smiled.

Suddenly the smirk returned and he took a step forwards, backing Kendall up against the dresser. There was virtually no space between them.

"Y'know, Princess, I kind of saved you today. If you're looking to reward my nobility, I think I have something in mind," he said, looking down at the lace still in her hand.

Kendall felt the air evaporate from her lungs as her face went red hot.

He gazed down at her, his dark blue eyes pulling her into a trance. She felt lust enveloping her as he licked his lips slowly.

She hated how much she loved it when he had her in the palm of his hand like this. She wished she could do the same to him and regain control.

She leaned into him, so their chests were touching and looked up through her lashes, slowly switching her gaze from his eyes to his lips. She smirked slightly as she felt something against her leg.

Without warning, she sidestepped out of his grasp and sat down on the edge of the bed, rummaging through her bag for her books so they could study.

Daniel turned round, looking mildly pissed, with his tongue in his cheek.

Once facing her, he looked down, his eyebrows raised.

"Quit staring at me, we have studying to do," Kendall said, looking down at the large tent in his pants. "What happened there, Daniel?" she said cheekily, feigning innocence.

He rolled his eyes, suppressing a grin and flopped down on his back beside her, leaning back on the headboard with his hands behind his head. He wasn't even bothering to hide it.

"I found out you're a tease, Princess, that's what happened," he said, accusingly.

She gasped dramatically and put her hand on her heart, feigning hurt. "Whatever do you mean? I think you just find me very attractive."

Daniel chuckled. "Allow me to fill you in on a little secret Princess...

Every man under the sun finds you very attractive," he stated assuredly.

Kendall looked down nervously, feeling her face grow hot, as it always did around Daniel.

"Even you?" she asked quietly.

Daniel looked completely serious, "Especially me."

Kendall felt her heart stop.

***

Kendall looked left and right as she walked cautiously down the large staircase ahead of Daniel. She was practically tiptoeing to avoid alerting Austin that she had a boy in the house.

They were a metre from the front door when she heard someone clear their throat. Kendall gulped and slowly turned around.

Austin stood in the large foyer, his arms crossed. Daniel looked unfazed as always.

"You're sneaking him in and out of the house?" Austin raised an eyebrow.

"I didn't sneak him in but I didn't necessarily want you to know about it," Kendall said, nervously rocking back on the balls of her feet.

"We were just studying, man," Daniel said casually.

Austin's expression darkened.

"Do you think I'm stupid? School was out three hours ago, you're wearing his clothes and now you're sneaking him out of the house," Austin said.

Kendall's eyes widened, "What are you implying?"

"Isn't it obvious? He thinks we've been fucking in your room for the past three hours," Daniel shrugged.

Austin grunted and if possible, his expression got even angrier. He took a step forward but Kendall stepped in between them.

"Relax," she snapped.

"First of all, who I do and do not sleep with is absolutely none of your business! But regardless, you've got it all wrong," Kendall said. Austin's look was sceptical, but he didn't interrupt.

"I had volleyball tryouts today after school, I made the team by the way."

"Oh, congratulations," Austin added.

"Thanks."

There was an awkward pause.

"Anyways, Daniel waited for me in the library as I intended to tutor him for an hour afterwards, so I was already going to be home two hours late. But then your psycho ex-girlfriend decided to steal my clothes, so Daniel came to my rescue with some spare clothes from his car. Then we decided to come back here to study and that's what we've been doing in my room ever since."

Austin's aggressive breathing gradually calmed down.

"Oh," Austin said.

Kendall laughed humourlessly.

"Yeah, *oh*, is correct."

"I'm sorry for overreacting," Austin said, looking down.

"Whatever," Kendall shrugged.

Austin looked up but this time his eyes were trained on Daniel who stood silently behind Kendall.

"Ken, why don't you say goodbye to your friend. I'd like to have a chat with him before he goes." Austin was deadly serious.

Chapter 25

Kendall rolled her eyes, "No, Aussie, you're not doing this right now."

"Ken, say goodbye," Austin said firmly.

Kendall stomped her foot.

"You're so embarrassing, ugh!" she whined and turned to Daniel. "Hopefully see you at school tomorrow, bye."

Daniel chuckled and gave her a wave as she reluctantly plodded upstairs. Once they heard her bedroom door click, they turned to face each other.

"You've never liked me, have you?" Daniel said.

Austin chuckled, "What I think of you is irrelevant."

Daniel furrowed his eyebrows in confusion, clearly having expected the *'stay away from my sister you dirtbag'* speech.

Austin sighed, "Look, regardless of what I think of you, I know where this is going. I can wag my finger in both your faces and tell you to stay away from each other but at the end of the day that won't achieve anything.

"You can deny it, but I can see you like her, even if you haven't admitted it to yourself yet. The thing that worries me is that Kendall doesn't have it easy. She puts up a good front, she never tells anyone when she's hurting but just rolls with the punches. She puts up with so much and I don't want her to have to put up with heartbreak as well, right now."

There was a pause as Daniel absorbed his words.

Austin went on. "You actually don't seem like the 'bad guy' everyone thinks you are. I don't mind you guys dating, I really don't, but she is the most important person in the world to me, so just don't ever make her cry, because then I'll have to make you cry."

Daniel chuckled. "I have no intention of ever making her cry, man. You don't have to worry."

Austin nodded and gave him a pat on the back, indicating he could leave.

***

The following day was chaotic, as if Kendall hadn't suffered enough the previous day.

As she and Ethan walked into school that morning, she got the surprise of her life.

She opened her locker door to face a super soaker that pelted her with water until her white top was completely saturated.

"Oh my god, what the hell was that?" Ethan exclaimed.

All around her, her peers were snickering, watching as she stood motionless, wearing a now see-through top!

Kendall grabbed her things from the locker, slammed the door shut and crossed her arms across her chest. She looked up at Ethan's outraged face.

"Why do you look so calm right now? Your locker just attacked you in broad daylight," he said, seemingly not suspecting the culprit.

Kendall laughed and rolled her eyes. "Don't be silly, E, this was Megan."

"Seriously? She has too much free time," Ethan said.

Kendall nodded as Ethan pulled his blue long sleeve shirt over his head, leaving him shirtless.

"What are you doing?" Kendall whisper shouted.

Girls around them weren't even trying to hide their stares.

He ignored the attention and thrust the shirt at her, nodding his head towards the girl's bathroom. Kendall realised he was telling her to go into the bathroom and change into his shirt.

"I can't let you spend the day shirtless, you'll get in trouble and you'll freeze," Kendall said.

Ethan shrugged, "I have a hoodie in my car. I'll go and get it if you go into the bathroom and change into the shirt."

Kendall giggled, "Thanks E, but you realise you could have just given me the hoodie and avoided the strip show."

He grinned cheekily, "I was just trying to improve the morale of the school this Thursday morning."

Kendall smiled sarcastically, "You're such a do-gooder."

"I try!" he said over his shoulder, as he made for the parking lot.

Kendall shook her head and laughed softly as she watched his retreating figure.

Once in the shirt she felt much better and certainly a lot warmer once she was out of the sopping wet Abercrombie shirt. She flung it into her locker and headed straight to first period where Daniel was waiting. He furrowed his brows at her oversized attire.

"Don't even ask," she said grumpily and slumped into her seat.

He put his hands up in surrender, looking amused already.

***

Fifth period was geography – not Kendall's favourite subject – so she'd started counting down the minutes from the moment she sat down.

She'd thought the water gun in her locker would be the worst part of her day, but Megan decided otherwise.

A boy named Andrew who was on the basketball team came and took his usual seat diagonally in front of Kendall. He then turned around to face her with a smirk which was slightly less normal.

Daniel's eyes were glued on his phone at this point.

"Hey Lockwood, sorry I missed the show this morning. It was nice of you to document it so us latecomers still got the full view." Andrew said condescendingly.

Kendall scrunched her face in confusion and turned to see if Daniel had understood but he was looking equally confused.

"What are you talking about?" Kendall asked.

Andrew lifted his phone and Kendall felt the whole world stop. The photo that had been mass texted to the entire school was of Kendall's locker and taped to it a picture of her wearing a completely see-through shirt, her black laced bra and cleavage on full display.

She snatched the phone as if that would delete the photo. But in reality, she knew the entire school would have this picture on their phones forever.

"Oh my god." Kendall muttered to herself, staring at the photo, her face in her hands.

"When did this happen? Wait- no, *how* did this happen?" Daniel asked.

"This morning! There was a super soaker in my locker, it saturated my shirt but I didn't realise she'd taken a photo! And I definitely didn't know she'd stuck it on my locker and sent it to the whole school," she said frantically. Then she paused as realisation hit her.

"It's still on my locker!" she yelled and bolted out of the classroom.

Chapter 26

She stormed through the hallway and felt like bursting into tears when she saw the crowd of laughing people surrounding her locker.

Wading through the crowd, she tore the paper off and stood for a moment, not wanting to turn round and see everyone cackling at her expense.

Hot with humiliation, she squeezed her eyes shut in an attempt to trap the tears but she couldn't stop the hot drops from tumbling down her cheeks. Tear after tear spilled out of her closed eyes.

Then she flinched at the booming voice behind her.

"Go to class, idiots!" Daniel's voice filled her ears.

The laughing subsided and people began to move away.

"Move!" his voice boomed again.

His scary bad guy privileges clearly worked; the hallway fell silent apart from his footsteps behind her. Furiously she wiped her cheeks and sniffed as quietly as possible, trying to hide her vulnerability.

A large hand gently turned her round and she looked up into Daniel's sympathetic smile.

"I'm sorry, Princess," he said softly.

She looked down, fighting the bile in her throat.

"You don't deserve this," he said, taking her hand in his.

His large rough hand enveloped her own and warmth filled her entire body.

Kendall gulped. "She's not going to stop," she said shakily. "It's only going to get worse."

Though her eyes were still cast down she could feel pity radiating from Daniel. Without a word, he brought her into his chest and wrapped his protective arms around her.

She stopped shaking and wrapping her arms around his torso, she nestled her head under his chin.

"Report her to the principal. Believe me, I'm the last person who goes to authority for help in my personal life, but the teachers actually like you at this school," he said, gently stroking her silky brown hair.

Kendall sighed, "Maybe, I don't know."

"You won't know unless you try. If they check the security footage they could get her and her clan suspended for this and for stealing your clothes yesterday," he said.

"Fine," she huffed.

***

Daniel was right.

After reporting the two incidents to the principal and insisting she check the security footage, Megan and her sheep were suspended for a week and a half. That meant at least a week and a half of peace for poor Kendall.

Daniel had agreed to help Kendall decide on a dress to wear to the wedding that weekend.

Kendall stepped out of the changing room in a gorgeous baby pink dress that fitted her like a glove. Her face however, was the opposite of satisfied.

"You okay, Princess?" he said looking up from his seat in the fitting rooms.

She nodded weakly and began to examine the dress unenthusiastically in the large mirror.

"You look incredible. Why do you look as if your puppy ran away?" he joked, trying to lighten the mood.

She stared at him, unimpressed. "I'm fine."

He quirked an eyebrow, urging her to tell the truth.

She sighed, "Everyone still has that photo on their phones."

Daniel sighed.

"I know, Princess, that sucks. Believe me when I say I'm not happy about it either," he said, angrily.

She looked curious, "Why are you pissed?"

He scoffed and leaned back, readjusting the position of his groin in his seat, and man-spreading his legs. His dark hair flopping over his eyebrows. Kendall cursed the butterflies in her stomach.

"Of course I'm pissed, you think I want the entire school to see what's mine?" he said with the cockiest of lopsided grins.

Chills ran through Kendall's body and her face turned hot. She hated him seeing how flustered he could make her. She knew she'd have to try and hide it.

She turned her nose up at him and raised her eyebrows snobbishly. "What's yours? What makes you think any part of me belongs to you?"

He chuckled and leaned forward to place his elbows in his thighs, then looked at her with a shit eating grin.

"Because, Princess, this weekend you're my fake girlfriend and I take my role *very* seriously," he said slowly.

Her knees were moments away from buckling, but she stood her ground, squaring her shoulders and flipping a few tendrils of hair over her shoulder.

"Dream on, Stryker. I belong to no one," she said confidently.

He raised a challenging eyebrow.

She had goosebumps and the hairs on the back of her neck stood up so fast you'd think they were baseball fans getting ready to hear the national anthem.

"I don't like this dress!" she blurted and disappeared back into the changing room.

She cursed her heart for skipping a beat at the beautiful sound of him laughing outside of the curtain. Everything he did seemed to send her into these frenzies, as if she had no control over herself whenever he was around.

***

After further analysis, she ended up getting the pink dress.

Once she had recovered from nearly being sent into cardiac arrest by Daniel being just too damn sexy, she'd looked in the mirror and seen that the dress was far too perfect for her just to put it back on the rack.

She wasn't a fan of the colour though, so she got it in a royal blue instead. This was against her better judgement though because she knew she loved the colour so much because it was the same blue as Daniel's eyes.

To her dismay, Daniel paid for it. The dress was $375 and he'd tapped his card before she could even open her wallet. She tried to fight him on it but he kept saying she was doing him a favour by attending this wedding and the least he could do was buy the dress.

"You hungry?" he asked as they walked out of the store and over to his car.

She looked up at him, "Kind of. What were you thinking?"

"That we could go and get food, dumbass."

She rolled her eyes as he opened the car door for her. "Well obviously. I meant did you have a particular place in mind?"

They both got in the car and he turned her with a grin.

"Always, Princess," he said with a wink, then turned on the engine and zipped out of the car park.

Chapter 27

They pulled up outside a small Italian restaurant that sat close to the beach. It looked warm and friendly with a picture of an overweight Italian man on the door saying 'Welcome!' in a speech bubble.

A bell above the door chimed as they walked in. Seeing them, a woman in an apron gasped and rushed over to Daniel, pulling him into a tight squeeze, ruffling his hair and peppering his face with kisses.

"My little Danny baby! How are you, kitten?" she gushed.

Kendall slapped her hand over her mouth to hide the explosive laughter threatening to engulf her.

Daniel nodded politely, "I'm all good, Debbie. How are you?"

Debbie giggled and ruffled his hair once more. "Oh, don't you worry about me, young man."

Try as she might, Kendall couldn't stop a giggle. Then Debbie noticed the brunette standing behind Daniel.

"And who is this gorgeous young lady? You can't be one of Danny's girls, you're way out of his league," Debbie said, winking and laughing along with Kendall.

Daniel forced a humourless laugh, "Very funny. Can you squeeze us in, Debs?"

She nodded smiling, grabbed some menus and took them to a corner booth.

Before Debbie could offer the menus, Daniel put out his hand.

"I'll have my usual, and so will my date," Daniel said confidently.

Debbie smiled knowingly and walked away.

Kendall's eyebrows flew up at the use of the word 'date'. She couldn't help the warm fuzzy feeling in her stomach.

"This is a date?" she asked, smirking.

He rolled his eyes, "It's easier if Deb thinks it is. She wouldn't believe me if I said it wasn't anyways."

Kendall nodded, disappointed by his answer.

He smirked at her slight frown, "Why, Princess? Do you want it to be a date?"

Kendall threw her napkin at him, "Shut up, Stryker."

Just then, Debbie came over with two diet cokes and two bowls of what looked like some incredible Italian pasta. She scurried off without a word but with an obvious Cheshire grin.

"Looks good," Kendall said.

"Dig in. It tastes even better than it looks."

"Just like me," he added, smirking.

Kendall scoffed, looking unimpressed at the dirty joke. He raised his eyebrows, waiting for her smile to crack.

Inevitably, the corners of her mouth twitched and she giggled, causing him to smile triumphantly.

"So how come she seems to know you so well?" Kendall asked, twirling pasta around her fork.

"I started working here when I was ten years old, washing dishes after school."

"Wow, that's pretty young. Why'd you need a job?"

He shrugged. "I was trying to impress my parents by showing my independence. Eventually, I gave up on that impossible mission and this place became a way to get financial separation from my parents. When I was 16, I got into fighting so I quit working here. I was making plenty of money through winning fights, but I still love to come here when I can."

Kendall gave him a sad smile. She knew how he felt, wanting so badly to be free of them that you'll do anything to escape the ties they have to you.

"It's a nice place. Besides, they seem to adore you here."

He chuckled, "Yeah, I guess they do. They're kind of like family."

They dove into their food, eating in comfortable silence.

"That was delicious," Kendall said, wiping her hands on her napkin.

"That's why it's my usual. Best dish on the menu," he said.

Kendall didn't think she'd have to try the entire menu to agree with him on that one.

"You want dessert?" he asked.

Kendall looked down at the large empty bowl and allowed food guilt to consume her. She swallowed down a sudden wave of nausea.

'You're already big enough, Darling. Why did you have to go and eat all of that?' Her mother's voice flooded through her thoughts.

She shook her head with a tight smile, "No thanks, I'm full."

He nodded and began looking through the dessert menu anyway. "Do you mind if I still get something? I'm not full yet."

Neither am I. She thought to herself.

"Go ahead," she nodded.

He ended up ordering the New York cheesecake and Kendall couldn't keep her eyes off of it.

Her mouth was practically watering when it was placed in front of him.

"You want to try some?" he asked politely.

She shook her head vigorously, "No thanks. Far too full."

"Are you okay?"

"Yes," she laughed nervously.

He looked at her concerned, "Why do I get the feeling that you're not telling me something?"

"Don't be silly. I'm fine," she insisted, looking around nervously.

Daniel knew she was bothered by something so he asked to get his cheesecake into a to-go box and took her back to his car. She tried to object to him paying but he left no room for discussion once again.

Once in the car Daniel made no move to start the engine.

"Look, you don't have to tell me if you don't want to, but please stop saying you're fine when you clearly aren't. I'm going to ask you one more time and if you want me to drop it then I will. What's wrong?" Daniel asked.

Kendall's eyes didn't lift from her lap as she twiddled her thumbs anxiously.

She wanted to give him answers, she really did, but she wasn't even sure what those answers were. She didn't have the words to even begin explaining what was wrong.

"You can tell me, Princess," he said just louder than a whisper.

The sincerity in his voice was enough to make her try to explain.

She took a deep breath whilst Daniel waited patiently.

"Sometimes, not all the time, I get this disgusting feeling during or after eating. I start to feel heavier by the second and then I just want to be sick. Sometimes I am. I don't really know what it is but I do know it's caused by my Mom and her sharp tongue.

"If making me feel like a beached whale on a daily basis was an Olympic sport, she'd be a gold medallist. Even when she's on the other side of the world, her insulting voice creeps into my brain and ruins my mood."

Daniel gazed over at the brunette next to him. Her answer made his chest feel tight.

"I'm sorry for ruining the mood," she brushed it off.

Daniel scoffed, "Shut up, Princess. I'm glad you told me. This has turned out to be a really great afternoon."

The corners of Kendall's mouth twitched.

"Yeah, it has," she said, finally looking up at Daniel.

Chapter 28

F riday meant a multitude of things:

1, the weekend was finally upon us.

2, leaving your school bag by the front door and napping for several hours,

3, homework because teachers are evil and like to ruin the luxury that is Saturdays and

4, house parties.

Number four was the only one applicable this Friday evening as Kendall and Chris dolled themselves up with perfect makeup, bouncy hair and skimpy outfits.

Chris was staying over at Kendall's house and had brought her entire wardrobe with her in order to choose what to wear for the party. She had also decreed that Kendall's outfit was far too conservative and Kendall needed some of her wise assistance.

Chris pulled out a tiny black slip dress with push up around the chest area. She viewed it with a knowing smirk and hurtled it at Kendall's head.

"Hey, you're gonna ruin my hair," Kendall whined, as she examined the dress.

"It's cute, right?" Chris waggled her eyebrows.

Kendall smiled.

"Yeah, so cute. Where's the rest of it?" she deadpanned.

"Come on, you'll look hot. Stryker won't be able to keep his hands off of you."

Kendall rolled her eyes, "Yeah, right."

"The best part is, the other guys won't be able to keep their eyes off of you either, and that will make Dan *loco*," Chris said, grinning.

Kendall held up the dress once more before storming into her closet to throw it on.

Chris chuckled.

***

Chris and Kendall entered the party with Ethan and Austin right behind them.

Thankfully, no one had got stuck with the designated driver job because the house was in the same neighbourhood as their own.

Austin leaned into Kendall's ear, "I'm really not liking that dress. I do not approve."

Kendall huffed, "I know, Aussie."

"And if any guys start giving you trouble or even just look at you for too long, I will make sure they leave with a broken nose," Austin said reassuringly.

Chris chuckled.

"Don't worry big man. Stryker will do that for you if ever you're not around," Chris said, giving him two thumbs up.

Austin and Ethan bid the girls farewell and went off to find their football buddies dispersed around the large house.

"Let's get wasted," Kendall said to Chris excitedly.

***

It didn't take long before Kendall and Chris were singing Adele's 'Someone like you' from the top of the kitchen island. Watching was a crowd of horny teenage boys, undoubtedly there just to catch a glimpse up the girls' skirts.

Trouble makers Daniel, Kai, and Blakes' arrival was perfectly timed.

Daniel plugged his ears to block the awful singing, then felt sick to his stomach when saw who it was.

Kendall's long tan legs in her black kitten heels were on full display, her dress was close to looking like lingerie and her perky breasts were practically spilling out of the top. She was holding onto an imaginary shared microphone with Chris and her hair was curly and messy as if she or someone else had just run their hands through it.

Daniel's jaw clenched. He was torn between being immensely turned on by this goddess in front of him, and wanting to punch the lights out of every guy staring at her as though she was their next meal.

Guys were leaning forward to look up the girls' skirts, surreptitiously touching their legs. Daniel was no longer in an internal dilemma.

Using both arms he shoved everyone aside and pulled Kendall off of the island, onto his shoulder, and then onto the ground, ignoring her drunken pouting protest. Blake had done the same with Chris and dragged her out of the room.

"Show's over," Daniel yelled at the guys still loitering.

"Oh, come on man, sharing is caring," some guy said, shamelessly ogling Kendall's legs.

Daniel abandoned what little self-restraint remained. The guy was on the ground in seconds and Kendall stood shocked, looking down at him.

"Let's go," Daniel said, taking her arm and pulling her outside onto the patio.

All the outdoor couches had people draped across them, smoking and drinking. Blake was talking quietly to Chris, seated on his lap. Daniel sat down beside him, attempting unsuccessfully to pull Kendall down too.

"I don't want to sit, I want to dance," she whined, pulling away from his grip.

"You can go dance in ten minutes once you've had a bit of fresh air. Sit down," he said firmly and leant back in his seat and with his legs apart.

She rolled her eyes and pouted, "I don't need fresh air. This is a party, Daniel, I want to go and da-"

She gasped as he cut her short and, grabbing her hips, pulled her onto his lap. Snaking an arm round her waist he pulled her close so that she was completely stuck if she tried to move.

"Don't test me right now, Princess," he whispered in her ear.

His breath on her neck, coupled with the feel of his arm around her waist, sent shivers down her spine.

"What is your problem? I didn't even do anything," she slurred.

He chuckled humourlessly, "I'm not mad at you. Not thrilled with you either because of your choice of clothing, or lack thereof."

Kendal knitted her eyebrows, "It's a party, Daniel. I wasn't keen on wearing a cloak. I think I look nice."

"You look more than nice. You look so hot it makes me want to bend you over this couch right now," he said agitatedly.

Her breath hitched in her throat and suddenly she felt as though her body was being drenched in lava.

"And that's the problem, Princess. Every guy here is having the same dirty thoughts as me. And it's making me pretty mad," he said, his words dripping in irritation.

Chapter 29

She was at a complete loss for words. She turned her head to hide her red hot face. The alcohol running through her veins was making her fidgety and much to Daniel's dismay, she began wriggling in his lap trying to get comfortable.

Blake and Chris chuckled as Daniel squeezed his eyes shut as if in pain. He groaned then grabbed Kendall's hips to keep her still.

He leaned closer, his mouth next to her ear.

"You need to stop moving," Daniel whispered.

"If I'm bothering you then I'll just head back inside to the dance floor," she said, making a move to stand up.

Daniel's hands reached out to pull her back down so that she was seated directly on his groin.

"I'm gonna need you to sit here for a couple more minutes after what you've done," he said firmly.

"What did I-" she stopped protesting when she felt something hard underneath her ass. Suddenly she understood.

"Oh," she said guiltily.

"Yeah, *oh*," he repeated.

Chris giggled, "Hey Lockwood, why don't you take him upstairs and help him out."

Kendall rolled her eyes dismissively and looked over at Daniel, expecting to see him doing the same. But Daniel was looking at her with a mischievous smirk and raised eyebrows.

Kendall was glad she had stayed seated as she was certain her knees would've buckled just from looking at that sexy smirk of his. Her body was so hot she was surprised Daniel's hands weren't getting burnt from where they were placed on her hips.

She felt like putty in Daniel's hands.

She scoffed, "Dream on, Stryker."

Daniel was about to say something else when a voice cut him off.

"Look who it is, my favourite Lockwood," Luke Cunningham's voice filled Kendall's ears and her heart dropped into her stomach.

She sighed and turned to look at Luke who had just sat down on the couch opposite. He looked her up and down, a menacing grin painted on his face. His shaggy blonde hair was falling over his forehead.

"Ugh," Kendall didn't even try hiding her distaste for the boy.

Luke's grin widened, "No need to bring out the claws just yet, save those for later."

She grimaced and felt Daniel tense beneath her as his demeanour became alert and angry.

"Who the hell is this guy?" Daniel said irritably, in a whisper only she could hear.

"He's a nobody," Kendall replied loudly, making sure Luke heard clearly.

The blonde boy's smirk faltered for a moment before he bounced right back, ready to provoke her further.

Kendall hoped Luke wouldn't ruin her night.

"Who's this new guy you've got, Ken?" Luke asked in a patronising tone.

"Piss off," she spat.

Luke chuckled, "You have no idea how much you turn me on when you talk like that."

He was interrupted as Daniel rose to his feet, pushing Kendall down behind him.

Luke didn't look half as frightened as Kendall knew he should be.

"Woah, calm down buddy. You and I have more in common than you might think," Luke said calmly, putting a hand up in between him and a fuming Daniel.

"Can we just go back inside please?" Kendall grabbed Daniel's arm and tried pulling him back inside before things escalated even further. Daniel gave Luke a warning glare before allowing Kendall to pull him away.

Luke clearly felt the need to add one final comment, "When am I gonna get another strip show from you, Ken?"

Kendall's eyes squeezed shut as she heard Daniel grunt and she braced herself for the chaos. He ripped away from her hold and took two large steps towards the blonde before sending a bone crushing punch straight into Luke's jaw.

The gathering crowd cringed at the painful blow that left Luke crumpled in a heap, knocked out cold.

Daniel was looking down at him with a dark glare and not even a hint of remorse.

Kendall's throat was dry and suddenly she was sober as a cobra.

She stormed past him and walked back into the house to grab water from the kitchen.

Daniel huffed and followed her inside guzzling half a litre of bottled water. People in the kitchen scattered the moment Daniel walked in so he could have some privacy with her.

"What the hell was that about back there? Who was that guy?" Daniel demanded, standing on the other side of the island.

Kendall looked at him in disbelief, "What do you mean *what happened*? You're the one who punched him."

"And what, you're mad about that?! What was I supposed to do, stand there and let him talk about you like that?!" Daniel said, raising his voice.

Kendall stayed silent, breathing heavily and glaring at him tempestuously.

Daniel took her silence as an opportunity to continue. "What was all that about anyway? You gave a strip show to that bleached chihuahua?"

Kendall huffed and looked down, not saying anything.

Daniel assumed she was confirming his suspicions by staying quiet, "Wait, you hooked up with that guy?"

"What? No! And will you quiet down!"

"Then tell me," he demanded.

"I don't owe you any kind of explanation. I already told you I didn't hook up with that guy. I already told you I had never kissed anyone before you, so I don't know why you would even suggest that! Besides, it's none of your business and you have no right to be angry at me right now," Kendall furiously whisper shouted then stormed out of the kitchen and up the stairs.

Daniel sighed as he watched her go.

Chapter 30

H e knew he had screwed up the moment he saw her retreating figure. He knew she probably wouldn't want to see him straight away, but he also knew a girl like her wasn't safe at parties like this by herself.

So he headed straight for the stairs to go and find her.

After checking every bedroom and bathroom, and being yelled at by angry naked people, he was beyond confused as to where she could have gotten to. He knew he saw her come up the stairs and had never seen her go back down.

Then another set of doors at the end of the hallway caught his attention. He was mentally face palming at how he hadn't thought to look at them, considering they were glass doors.

They led to a balcony where a small brunette girl was seated on the stony floor, her long legs dangling between the black metal fencing. Her hair was flowing softly in the breeze and her eyes gazed wistfully into the stars. She hugged the fencing in front of her and swung her dangling legs.

Daniel clicked open one of the doors. Kendall didn't even look up at the intrusion.

He took a moment to take her in. Never had he seen an image so beautiful; like a vinyl cover for a sad song.

Daniel sat down beside her with his back against the metal fence and his legs stretched. He looked over at Kendall. She pretended not to notice him.

"I'm sorry," Daniel said.

She didn't acknowledge him at all, but kept staring into the moonlight.

"I wasn't mad at you. I'm not mad at you. I was mad at all of those guys for talking about you and treating you like some object. I'm sorry I yelled," he said sincerely.

Kendall turned her head to look at him. She looked tired, but not in need of sleep, just tired.

Daniel sighed looking at her guiltily, "It makes me so crazy when people talk about you like that. I knew that guy was just looking for trouble and I still rose to it. I shouldn't have taken that out on you."

Kendall nodded in understanding, "I'll forgive you."

Daniel breathed a sigh of relief.

"If... you admit that you were jealous," Kendall smirked.

He looked at her in disbelief, "Are you serious right now?"

She nodded excitedly.

He rolled his eyes, "Fine."

Kendall raised her eyebrows expectantly.

He huffed and looked straight ahead, avoiding her eyes

"Maybe I was a little bit jealous," he said.

Kendall quirked an eyebrow as if to say '*not good enough*'.

He noticed and huffed again.

"Fine, I was really jealous," he said looking down, embarrassed.

Kendall grinned from ear to ear. "Aw, you were jealous," she cooed.

"Shut up," he chuckled.

She giggled along, loving being the one in control for once.

He suddenly remembered something.

"Wait, so what was the strip show he was referring to? Or did he just make that up to piss me off?" he asked curiously.

Kendall looked away, annoyed.

"I'm not insinuating anything I promise. I'm just genuinely confused," he added.

She exhaled nervously, "It's kind of a long story."

Daniel leaned back and put his hands behind his head, "I've got time."

Kendall swallowed her nerves and dove into the story from when the previous year she had worn the incorrect sized uniform and practically flashed both teams.

***

They spent the next two hours on that balcony.

They talked and laughed and just enjoyed one another's company. They also established further details for the wedding the following day, like what time he was collecting her, sleeping arrangements, etc.

Eventually, after Kendall almost fell asleep sitting up, headed back downstairs.

Chris and Blake greeted them and they all decided to head home. Chris was staying over at Kendall's and despite it being less than a ten-minute walk, Blake and Daniel refused to let them go alone.

At the front door, Blake gave Chris a passionate kiss goodbye while Daniel gave Kendall stood awkwardly looking on.

Once they finally broke apart and bid farewell. Chris rushed inside, muttering something about 'bedtime'.

Blake chuckled and strolled slowly out of the driveway. Daniel walked backwards slowly, grinning widely at Kendall as he went.

"See you for the big day, Princess. Nine AM sharp!" he said cheerfully.

Kendall nodded, smiling at his stupid grin.

Once both of the guys were out of view, she made her way inside and up to her bedroom where Chris was waiting.

She was under the covers in a giraffe onesie with a huge child-like grin.

"You know when I first met you, I never would have thought you were a giraffe onesie kind of girl," Kendall said, amused.

"Don't make this about my sleeping attire, Mija. What happened with you and Stryker tonight?" Chris asked knowingly.

Kendall began changing into her pyjamas, looking away from Chris to hide her excited smile. Once she was cosy inside the silk material and happily removing her makeup with a cotton pad, she turned to look at the impatient giraffe in her bed.

"We talked," Kendall stated.

Chris raised an eyebrow. "Talked? About what?"

Kendall shrugged, "I don't even really know. Nothing, everything."

Chris began excitedly convulsing as she giggled and wiggled in the bed with scrunched eyes and a toothy grin. Kendall looked at her concerned.

"That's so romantic!" Chris blurted.

Kendall chuckled, "Is it?"

"One second you were yelling at him and the next second you guys are pouring your life stories out to one another on a balcony under the stars." Chris looked up as she imagined it, placing her hands on her heart and sighing dramatically.

"Did that ever happen with you and Blake?" Kendall asked, taking a seat on her side of the bed.

"Don't change the subject!" Chris snapped, pointing her finger in Kendall's face.

Kendall put her arms up in surrender. "Sorry. I just think you guys are so cute. I want to know how you crazy kids got together."

"Story for another time, darling," Chris said softly.

Kendall sighed, disappointed.

"Please just admit that you like him," Chris asked hopefully.

Kendall looked at her sheepishly.

"Well, I've never liked anyone before. So how do I know if that's what I'm feeling? I mean, I like being around him. He makes me laugh a lot. He's actually really smart and he listens to me which I really appreciate. He always makes me feel heard.

"I sometimes think he kind of looks at me like I'm important to him, which I don't feel I get from anyone else. But when I get it from him, he makes everyone else not matter anymore. I can't deny that I miss him when he skips school, or that I worry when he gets hurt.

"I just like whatever it is that we have and I don't want to lose him by complicating things and maybe scaring him off.".

Chris looked like she was very close to tears. "Oh, my baby Ken, you don't just like this man.

You *love* him."

Chapter 31

K endall's alarm blared painfully loud at the ass crack of dawn. Her phone read 7:30 am.

It very quickly became evident that Chris is not a morning person when she punched the alarm clock halfway across the room without so much as lifting her head off of the pillow.

Kendall begrudgingly dragged herself into the shower, forced herself to pack, do her makeup and hair, and put together a half decent pre-wedding outfit that would be comfy enough for the two-hour journey to the hotel.

She told Chris she could stay as long as she liked and let herself out whenever she wanted to leave. She bid her farewell and headed outside into the early morning Rhode Island breeze.

Daniel was leaning against his black car in the driveway, looking devilishly handsome as always. He stood with his arms crossed, making his muscles bigger than Kendall's head. He wore a navy hoodie, dark blue jeans and of course his signature bad boy smirk as he saw her approaching.

"Morning, Princess."

"Mornin'," she grunted.

He chuckled at her grumpiness.

"Just so you know, I will be sleeping for this entire journey. I don't think you want me being a bitch to your parents because of sleep deprivation, so it's in both our best interests really," Kendall said, piling into the front seat after he had taken her bags and put them in the trunk.

He shut the trunk and joined her up front.

"As long as you don't snore," he teased.

Kendall looked at him blankly and weakly shook her head.

"Then snooze away," he said, chuckling. The deep sound gave Kendall butterflies.

***

The hotel was glorious. White marble floors and columns with gold floral decor.

They hadn't even entered the wedding venue area of the building and Kendall already felt this was the most gorgeous room she'd ever seen.

She zoned out completely whilst Daniel got them checked in at the front desk. She was too enamoured by her surroundings to pay any attention. Eventually, a bell boy took their bags and headed into the golden elevator.

The ride was painfully silent. Daniel kept looking down at her with an amused grin as they both tried their best not to start laughing uncontrollably. They weren't even sure why they felt so inclined to laugh.

At last, they made it to their room and they parted ways with the bellboy. They opened the door to the room and Kendall's eyes widened.

One bed.

She laughed internally at the predictability of her situation.

Daniel seemed unsurprised by the individual king-sized bed in the room as he sauntered in without a care in the world, dropping the bags into the corner.

"Urm, why did you book us a room with one bed?" Kendall said, entering the room.

Daniel turned to face her, grinning.

"Don't flatter yourself, Princess. I didn't book the rooms. My parents did. And obviously with them thinking we're a couple, they saw no issue with a double bed," he sounded amused by the whole situation.

Kendall scowled.

He moved to stand directly in front of her and placed his hands on her shoulders, "Come on, it'll be fine. I know this is your first time sharing a bed with a guy but don't worry, I'll make it an unforgettable experience," he winked at the last part.

Goosebumps formed on her skin but she ignored the tingling feeling.

She shrugged off his hands, "Take a cold shower, Stryker," she said walking over to her suitcase to start getting ready.

She heard him chuckle behind her.

"Yes ma'am," he said.

Just then, the bathroom door clicked shut.

She heard the shower turn on and couldn't resist the amused grin that spread across her face. He had actually followed her instructions to go and have a cold shower.

Unbelievable.

***

After having to beg Daniel to get out of the shower when he had taken thirty minutes doing God knows what, she was finally able to get near the bathroom mirror and start work on her face and hair.

Whilst doing so she had to try relentlessly to think about anything but the jaw dropping image of Daniel walking out of the bathroom dripping wet with a white towel hanging dangerously low on his hips. His chiselled abs and v-line were on full display and glistening from the water droplets on his tanned skin.

Not an easy task to say the least.

A short while later, she was ready, hair bouncy, makeup pristine, kitten heels equipped, and royal blue dress hugging her in all the right places.

She took a deep breath and opened the door to the bedroom, and could not have anticipated the sight she walked in on.

Daniel, clad in nothing but black Calvin Klein boxers, was stretched out on his back, looking at his phone in one hand with the other resting behind his head.

Kendall gulped.

He noticed her arrival and looked up from his phone, smirking and looking her up and down hungrily.

She fought the urge to do the same to him.

"Blue was definitely the right colour choice. I can't wait to have you on my arm tonight, everyone is going to be so jealous of me," he said huskily, his eyes still trained on her legs.

She felt her cheeks reddening but before she could cave with embarrassment, she snapped herself out of it and looked at him impatiently.

"Why aren't you ready?" she asked in a clipped tone.

He chuckled and stood up. Kendall reluctantly cast her eyes to the wall.

"Relax, Princess. All I have to do is jump into my suit. It'll take two minutes," he said as he unzipped the dry-cleaning bag.

"Why did you not get dressed whilst I was in the bathroom?"

"The look in your eyes when you walked in told me that you liked what you saw. I wouldn't deprive you of that," he said buttoning up his shirt.

Kendall narrowed her eyes whilst silently thanking his charming intuition.

***

"Hold my bicep," Daniel said.

Kendall looked up at him strangely.

He rolled his eyes, "How do you expect people to believe we're a couple if you completely refuse to touch me."

Kendall huffed before begrudgingly linking her arm around his bicep. Daniel smirked back. He knew she was a ball of nerves.

They walked arm-in-arm into the venue and Kendall held back a gasp. The ceiling was impossibly high and was carved beautifully into swirls and patterns. She almost tripped over her own two feet as she stared up at it.

Daniel sighed nervously beside her.

"You know, Princess, I've been thinking. Maybe we don't need to pret"-

They seemed to be the last ones to enter as everyone else was already seated.

"We're late," she exclaimed, cutting him off.

Daniel huffed at the failed opportunity and guided her to the front row where his parents stood waiting to greet them. Kendall gulped down her anxiousness.

"Mom, Dad," Daniel nodded in greeting to them.

They nodded back, their expressions indifferent.

Kendall saw instantly where Daniel got his piercing blue eyes from, as the same ones stared back at her from his mother. She had thick blonde hair and fair skin. Daniel also seemed to get his sharp jawline from her. From his father, he seemed to have inherited only the same fluffy dark hair. They didn't share many other similarities apart from maybe their tall height.

They were clearly people of power; Kendall sensed a judgemental air, similar to that her mother usually had around strangers. Well actually, Mrs Lockwood was usually at her most judgemental when her daughter was around.

Kendall sensed the tension between Daniel and his parents by their uncomfortable stances.

"I want you to meet my girlfriend, this is Kendall Lockwood," Daniel said formally.

Kendall fought the adoring smile that threatened to make its way onto her face when he called her his girlfriend. She could listen to him call her that over and over again.

She shook herself out of her daze, outstretched her hand and smiled brightly. To her surprise, Mr and Mrs Stryker returned the same warmth and shook her hand enthusiastically.

"What a pleasure! How did my son get a gorgeous girl like you? Your mother and I are great friends," Mrs Stryker said cheerfully.

Kendall's heart melted slightly at the surprisingly nice greeting and she felt a wave of relief at their acceptance of her.

***

The ceremony was peaceful and beautiful. The vows almost brought Kendall to tears but she refused to let one spill.

After the happy couple walked down the aisle arm in arm, they all headed to the reception. Kendall found herself chit chatting with Mrs Stryker for more than twenty minutes.

"So where are you headed to college in the fall?" Mr Stryker chimed in after having stayed silent throughout the conversation.

"Bob, don't interrogate the poor girl."

He continued to look at Kendall as though waiting for an impressive answer.

"Princeton," Kendall said with a tight smile.

Mr Stryker's eyebrows rose in surprise.

"Impressive."

Kendall nodded awkwardly and scanned the room for any sign of Daniel. She eventually spotted him on one of the other tables, seemingly not enjoying the conversation he was having with some man.

Mrs Stryker interrupted her thoughts, "You know, Kendall, It's so nice to see Daniel with a girl like you. I've been waiting for the right girl to come along and really whip him into shape. He's been such trouble all these years and I was worried he might never change. But now his grades are up, he's not skipping school, he's pleasant, not to mention I haven't seen him with a cigarette since he first came home and told us he got a new tutor. You've really changed him for the better, Kendall. Thank you for that."

Kendall's heart fluttered at Mrs Stryker's acceptance and gratitude. However, a wave of anger consumed her at the emphasis on Daniel needing to *change*.

"With all due respect, Mrs Stryker, I believe you've had a wonderful and pleasant son under your nose this whole time. I may be responsible for motivating him to apply himself in school, but the surge of increase in his grades is all down to him. He is a lot smarter than you give him credit for. He is also insanely charming and very respectful. I think maybe you've been looking for the worst in him for too long, because the good in him really isn't hard to see. I hope I didn't overstep," Kendall said nodding, before excusing herself and heading over to the table Daniel was seated at.

When she reached him, the man he was talking to looked up and smiled. She noted some obvious similarities to Daniel.

The man reached his hand out to shake hers politely, "I'm Ben, the older brother. It's nice to finally meet the girl Daniel has been bragging about so much."

Kendall chuckled and shook his hand, "Oh, really?"

"He's embellishing," Daniel brushed it off.

"Whatever you say, brother. Kendall, why don't you take my seat, I should really go and mingle," Ben offered before bidding a farewell and disappearing into the swarm of people.

Kendall was about to drop down into the seat but Daniel had other plans and pulled her onto his lap instead. Kendall squeaked slightly at the surprise manoeuvre and was about to jump up and tell him off when she realised that wouldn't be very 'girlfriendly' of her.

He moved her in his lap so she was able to face him fully.

"I like you better right here, Princess," Daniel said softly.

Her brain became foggy.

"Yeah, I'm sure you do, Stryker," she huffed and made herself comfortable in his lap.

She felt him tense beneath her and suck in a breath. She silently chuckled.

"So how come your brother is such a delight?" Kendall asked.

Daniel raised his eyebrows, "Are you saying that I'm *not* a delight?"

"Well, It's not one of the first words that comes to mind if I were to try and describe you."

Daniel smirked, "What words would you use? Handsome, rugged, charming, sexy?"

She giggled, "Well, I would definitely start by describing you as *modest*."

"Oh, yeah, that too," he smiled cheekily.

She chuckled as she looked at his gorgeously chiselled face and felt herself falling into his smoky blue eyes.

"Will you try not to blush and look away if I tell you that you're beautiful?" he said looking deeply into her eyes.

A wide smile took over her face and butterflies flew cheerfully in her stomach. She felt herself melting into his hands when he looked at her like that.

Like she was important to him.

"And that smile. God, I wish I could make you smile all day, every day, just to see those dimples," he said grinning at her.

That was the breaking point for her and against her will, her cheeks flamed and she broke eye contact.

"I tried," she said, giggling softly.

"You did," he said, also chuckling.

They both sobered up and gazed into each other's eyes once more.

"I tried to ask you earlier but..." he began.

Kendall grew nervous.

"I wonder, why don't we just not pre-"

He was cut off by his sister Ellen who pulled Kendall off of his lap.

"Time to dance!" she exclaimed and dragged Kendall away from a bewildered Daniel who had lost yet another chance to tell her how he felt.

Kendall sent him an apologetic smile.

Chapter 32

D aniel stared longingly at the dance floor where Kendall swayed, her hips and arms moving rhythmically to the beat.

Her carefree smile made Daniel jealous that he wasn't the person causing it.

It brought him back to one of their first ever interactions when she was dancing with Kai at his party. It was barely a month ago but it felt like centuries. He vividly remembered the insane jealousy he'd felt watching her in his best friend's arms. Daniel chuckled at how delusional he'd been back then to have denied his burning crush on her. No matter how many people around him saw it, he could never quite piece it together himself.

As he watched her dance without a care in the world, he realised he had been falling for her from the moment she walked into the Principal's office. Daniel smiled at the memory of how she had blushed like crazy the first time he'd called her 'Princess'.

Eventually, fifty songs later, the tone of the party changed and a slow song came on. Couples gathered in the centre of the floor, holding each other and swaying slowly to the sound of 'Give me love' by Ed Sheeran.

Kendall turned to Daniel with a pleading look, holding out her hand to him.

He sighed, caving instantly. Taking her hand, he guided her to the centre of the room, where they were hidden amongst the other couples.

He placed his hands on her waist and she linked hers at the back of his neck, softly combing through the hair she could reach. He felt his defences crumble at her touch.

They began their gentle swaying to the romantic song, staring into each other's eyes as if their lives depended on it. Suddenly there was no one else in the room, just the two of them and the sound of Ed Sheeran.

Daniel's mouth turned up into a smile as he looked down at the beautiful girl in his arms. He wanted to laugh out loud at his predicament. If you had told him a month ago he'd be falling hard and fast for Kendall Lockwood as they slow danced, he would have told you to seek professional help.

But as he analysed the situation and the setting, he didn't understand how he hadn't seen this coming. He had always seen her in the halls or as being a know-it-all in class, and he had always known she was beautiful. But he had never anticipated that getting to know her properly, more than just at surface level, would make such a difference. He supposed that was naive of him.

"What's going on in that head of yours?" she said, bringing him out of his thoughts.

He chuckled softly, looking down at her confidently, "You."

She became visibly nervous and giggled anxiously.

"What about me?" Kendall asked.

"Well, I've been trying to tell you something all day, but I kept getting interrupted," Daniel said.

She made a face that told him to continue.

He sighed, "I don't want to pretend."

Kendall's head tilted to the side.

"I don't want to pretend that you're my girlfriend and I want to stop acting like there isn't something going on between us," he continued.

She looked slightly windswept. As if he had unlocked a door she wasn't quite ready to open.

Her hesitation didn't deter his perseverance.

He sighed again, "I like you, Kendall."

Kendall's breath was completely stolen from her and her eyes smiled. She blinked up at him in complete disbelief.

For a second she looked almost sad, "Why?"

His face twisted in confusion, "What do you mean *why*?"

She raised her eyebrows, urging him to answer. It was as if the prospect of someone liking her was absolutely unfathomable.

"How could I not? You're quite literally the most perfect person I've ever met. You're intelligent, hard-working, athletic, caring, generous, funny, and do have to mention, the most beautiful women I have ever laid eyes on. You aren't afraid to put me in my place and it drives me insane.

"I like who I am when I'm with you. The only complaint I have is that you're not mine and I won't be happy until you are," he finished, quirking an eyebrow.

She took a deep breath, tempted to pinch herself to check if she was dreaming. He stared down at her adoringly.

She believed him.

She never thought she would believe someone when they said something like that but he'd managed to break down her walls and look her straight in the eyes.

She jokingly rolled her eyes, "Well, if your happiness depends on it, then I suppose I will throw you a bone," she smiled cheekily.

He smirked and crashed his lips onto hers. Her arms wound around his neck and ran through his soft brown hair.

She kissed him so passionately that she was struggling to breathe. His arms clutched her waist and she was certain her knees would give way if he were not holding her so tight.

She deepened the kiss, wanting as much of him as possible. Nothing was enough. Every firework going off inside of her just made her hungry for more, never satisfying the want she had to have every piece of him.

He seemed to be struggling with the same problem as they both fought for dominance in the kiss.

Kendall was aware that what they were doing was probably very inappropriate in the middle of someone else's wedding reception. They broke apart, leaning their foreheads against each other as they both tried to catch their breath.

They panted softly as they held each other in comfortable silence, processing everything.

"I'm gonna go out on a limb here and guess that maybe you like me too?" Daniel piped up jokingly.

"Shut up."

"I want to hear you say it," he said.

She rolled her eyes, "Daniel."

"Yes?" he said, looking down at her expectantly.

She huffed. He smirked.

"Fine, moron. Maybe, I like you too," she said.

His smirk widened and he leaned in to give her a long peck on the lips.

Her heart soared.

"All I want to do is kiss you right now," he admitted.

"What's stopping you, Stryker?" she looked up at him enticingly.

"Not here," he stated before taking her hand in his.

He pulled her with him out of the large room and out into the hallway that was full of people. They were looking around for any kind of deserted area where they could make out like the love sick teens they were.

Unfortunately, there were plenty of other people littering the hall-ways and even the lobby.

They both sighed.

"We've still got our hotel room," Daniel said.

Kendall knew how that sounded but she was beyond caring. She wasn't about to pretend she wasn't completely okay with going to that hotel room and happily see where it led them.

So that's what they did.

Chapter 33

The sun streamed in through the large windows and cast an amber glow over the room.

Kendall's eyes fluttered open, squinting in the brightness. She rolled over to protect her retinas and came face to face with a sleeping Daniel.

The light glistened on his smooth skin and his fluffy brown hair was tousled in all directions. His expression was neutral and peaceful. His arms were wrapped around Kendall's naked waist which brought her back to the events of the night before. She smiled softly as she looked at his perfect face.

"You're staring," he suddenly spoke in a groggy voice, startling Kendall.

She cleared her throat to recover from being blatantly caught out. He kept his eyes closed.

"Why would I stare at something so ugly," she said playfully.

He opened his eyes slowly.

Before Kendall could take back what she said, Daniel was on top of her with his face barely an inch from hers.

"I'm struggling to believe that you find me ugly considering the things you let me do to you last night," he said cockily. His raspy morning voice sent chills through her body.

Kendall blushed and smiled cheekily, "I don't recall?"

Daniel smirked and moved his mouth over to her ear to whisper, "You don't recall screaming my name?"

Kendall's body was suddenly hot and alert. Shivers ran through every nerve.

"Maybe you need reminding," he said darkly before pulling the covers over them both.

***

The drive home was a peaceful one. After saying goodbye to everyone and hitting the road, Kendall was already exhausted.

She was out like a light before Daniel even turned the car on and he was quite happy to let her sleep as he digested the events of the weekend.

Just as they arrived at Kendall's house, she realised with a shock that her mother had returned home. Her car was parked outside the house. "STOP!" she yelled, just in time to prevent Daniel from pulling into the driveway. The car came to a screeching halt.

"What's wrong?!" Daniel yelled back, extremely concerned.

"My mother can't see you dropping me off. I have to get out right here," Kendall said frantically and began undoing her seatbelt.

Daniel seemed confused, "Why?"

"She's super critical of everything I do. She'll never approve of me having a boyfriend unless she handpicked him herself. It's not you, I just really don't want her chewing me out right now," Kendall said.

Daniel's features relaxed and he nodded before helping to get her things out of the trunk.

He gave her a long peck on the lips as a goodbye.

"See you tomorrow in school, Princess," Daniel said smugly.

"Bye, Daniel," she sang over her shoulder and made her way to the driveway.

She opened her front door and felt her heart drop into her stomach.

Her mother was standing in the foyer, arms crossed and with a deadly glare trained on her daughter.

"Ah, here's the liar," her mother said.

Kendall dropped her bags and looked at her mother with alarm.

"Where've you been? And don't try lying to me because I already know the answer," Mrs Lockwood said, stepping closer.

"Mom, what's wrong?" Kendall said as dread weighed on her like a blanket of metal chains.

Her mother's expression darkened, "*What's wrong*?! What's wrong is that I just got a call from Mrs Stryker telling me she's delighted to hear that my daughter is *dating* her son!"

Kendall's eyes widened.

"Yeah! And that's not all. She also mentioned how it was lovely to finally meet you this weekend at her daughter's wedding?!" she bellowed.

Kendall suddenly felt the urge to throw up as her panic rapidly increased.

"I have been waiting and *pining* for a man to finally settle for you and when you finally pick one yourself... you pick *him*?"

Settle for you, Kendall repeated in her head. Tears welled in her eyes.

"This is why I was taking it upon myself to find people *for* you. I always knew your taste would be catastrophic."

Red hot anger consumed Kendall upon hearing such disrespect towards Daniel.

Her mother didn't stop there, "They are a respectable family I'll give you that. But they have *two* sons, Kendall. *Two*. Why did you have to go and pick the lowlife that will only use you to get you on your back. Honestly, you can be so stupid sometimes. You will break up with that troublemaker by the end of the day."

Kendall's fear and dread dissipated and was replaced with blinding rage.

"No!" Kendall snapped.

Her mother looked like she was choking on a grape.

"Wha- no?!"

"I said no!" Kendall repeated.

Mrs Lockwood looked at a complete loss for words.

"Do you even hear yourself?" Kendall said.

"I suggest you watch your tone with me child!" her mother said, making another attempt at being intimidating.

But gone was the frail girl that cowered at her mother's feet.

"I'm not a child. I'm 18. You would know that if you were here on mine and Austin's birthday on September 1st. But don't worry, I didn't miss you. In fact, I never miss you. When you are here, I'm just counting down the minutes until you are gone again. How can you even call yourself a mother?"

Mrs Lockwood looked seconds away from bursting into flames. She stormed over to Kendall and swung her right backhand to her daughter's face. Kendall's left cheek seared with pain as she held back a sob. She turned her head back to face the woman before her and felt warm liquid dripping down her cheek from where her mother's ring had pierced her skin.

The blood she'd inflicted on her daughter's face clearly wasn't enough for her because she then slammed her up against the door. Kendall, winded by the impact, realised her mother had finally resorted to violence.

"I HAVE GIVEN YOU EVERYTHING MONEY CAN BUY! I RAISED YOU!" Mrs Lockwood roared hysterically.

Kendall looked up at her mother defiantly, hiding the pain in her back from hitting the door and the pain in her heart she had bottled up for years.

"I raised myself!" Kendall spat out, her eyes blurring as the tears fought to break the surface.

Silence.

Her mother looked at her with pure hatred.

"Did you know I got into Princeton? Did you even know that I applied? Did you know I'm captain of the Volleyball team? Or that I have the highest GPA in school? No, you didn't. You claim to have raised me yet you know nothing about me," Kendall said calmly.

Still nothing from her mother.

"You don't get to pull out the 'mother card' whenever it's convenient anymore. I have been so blinded by your opinion of me for years that I actually believed it myself. Daniel has finally opened my eyes to the love and appreciation that has always been there and I will not allow you to take him away from me," Kendall said confidently.

"Enough!" Mrs Lockwood cried.

Kendall took a deep breath and continued, "You know I've realised why you treat me with such animosity. I've seen the way Grandma treats you and how you cower when she's around. I bet you resent her beyond belief because she has made you feel inadequate your entire life. I bet she zoomed in on every flaw and every mistake. Has she ever told you that she's proud of you? Has she ever even told you that she *loves* you?"

Her mother began sputtering incoherently.

"So now you use your daughter as a way to turn the tables, so you're the one in with the power to make someone else feel as small as she made you. You couldn't rise above what she did to you so instead you grew bitter and did the same to me. That doesn't make you powerful, it makes you weak. You're the most pathetic person I have ever met," Kendall spat.

Mrs Lockwood was close to tears as she stared down at her daughter in shock. Kendall took her silence as a win and moved out from in between her and the door, grabbed her bags off of the floor and headed out the front door without looking back.

Chapter 34

Daniel arrived home late that afternoon and slumped into the couch. His family was not yet back, so he was home alone.

A small grin spread across his face as he thought about Kendall, the woman who had been the centre of every thought and dream he'd had since the moment he first spoke to her on that first day of senior year.

His daydreaming was interrupted by the ringing of the house phone. He huffed in annoyance and reaching over to the side table beside the couch, he put the phone to his ear.

"Daniel Stryker, this is Mrs Lockwood," a sharp voice came through the line.

He suddenly felt on edge.

"Yes?" he said sceptically.

"I'm going to say something very quickly Daniel, and I need you to pay attention. Can you do that Daniel?"

His jaw clenched at the use of his full name by anyone other than Kendall.

"Okay," he said through gritted teeth.

"My daughter is on her way to your house to run into your arms and seek comfort after a rather chaotic argument that we just had. You are not going to hug or comfort her. You will break up with her in the most horrid and cold-hearted way so that she hates you and never wants to speak to you again."

His eyebrows scrunched in confusion and he grew angry.

"With all due respect, Mrs Lockwood, I'm going to have to pass on your tempting offer," he said sarcastically.

"It wasn't a request, Daniel. Your relationship with my daughter is dividing this family down the middle and I cannot have that. She has become defiant and disrespectful and I know it's because of you. If you don't do as I say as soon as she arrives at your house shortly, you leave me with no choice but to cut her off financially.

And don't think you can take her in and support her yourself. Her college tuition is eighty grand a year and that doesn't include books, food or accommodation. If you tell her about this predicament, you know she'll choose you over college and you know that's not what's best for her. Her future lies in your hands, Daniel.

And just in case you are as selfish as I think you might be and her future isn't enough to persuade you, I have something else I can take away from her. She has been curious about her father for as long as I can remember. If you take yourself out of her life, effective immediately, I will tell her everything I know about her father and where to find him, on the day she leaves for college.

Think of what you would be doing for her, Daniel. She would be able to find her father and get answers to all her questions, whilst also living out her life at Princeton university without a care in the world.

Don't make the wrong choice."

The line cut off and almost comically, the doorbell rang.

Daniel felt like he was being torn in ten different directions. Bile rose in his throat. He felt a rage he had never felt before. He was completely powerless. It didn't matter that he could render men twice his size unconscious with a single punch, this woman was ready for every skill and tactic he had under his belt.

He stood, erased every trace of emotion from his face, and slowly walked towards the front door.

His hand hovered over the handle for a moment as he squeezed his eyes shut and prepared himself for the hardest thing he would ever have to do.

He swung open the door and fought the urge to melt at the sight before him.

Kendall's tears welled over and wet tracks on her face told him she'd been crying the entire journey from her house. There was a cut on her left cheek surrounded by bright red drying blood. He desperately wanted to know what had happened whilst he tended her wounds, but he knew better than to ask.

She was distraught, her hair was messy and scrunched.

Daniel's heart wrenched and it took all his willpower not to scoop her up and stroke her better.

Without hesitation, she wrapped her arms around his middle and nestled her head into his chest. But his arms stayed by his side and he looked straight ahead as if his life depended on it.

Of course, it was now pelting with rain.

"Why are you here?" he croaked.

Kendall looked up, confused by his tone, and detached herself from his body.

"I got into an argument with my Mom. I needed to get out of there," she said shakily.

Daniel took a deep breath and prepared the knife he was about to stab and twist.

"I'm not doing this with you, Kendall," he said.

She looked at him, lost but hopeful.

"What?"

"Look, it was fun but now I've got what I wanted, so for the rest of high school it's probably best if we go back to being strangers." He was staring down at her with a stony expression.

In goes the knife.

"Where is this all coming from? I was with you like thirty minutes ago," she said through blurry eyes.

Now it's time to twist it.

"Don't you get it? I got what I wanted from you this weekend. If I had known all I had to do to get you into bed was to make up some bullshit speech about how much I like you, then I would've done it ages ago," Daniel said with a cruel smirk.

Kendall was at a complete loss. She cast her eyes to the ground and shook her head in disbelief.

"You don't have to tutor me anymore since I'm doing pretty well in all my classes, so we don't have to put up with each other's company everyday. Oh, and thanks for getting my parents off my back by the way." Every word sounded so sincere.

Kendall looked up from the ground and glared at him angrily.

"You were so desperate to get me into bed that you kept up an act for over a month? That's pathetic," she spat.

Daniel couldn't have agreed more, but he had to maintain the narrative.

"Don't be too disappointed, babe, you were a good lay," he said snidely.

Kendall's gaze softened and a tear tumbled down her cheek.

Daniel's heart tore straight down the middle as he watched her disintegrate before his eyes.

"You know what, Daniel, you really are a bad guy," she said wistfully then picked up her bags and walked down the driveway to her car.

Her words tore through him like a sword through a silk scarf. Daniel realised he had been twisting the knife into himself in the process.

Chapter 35

The school entrance towered over Kendall like a rickety haunted house with crows circling above in the purple sky. Her insides screamed at her to flee back to her car, but she knew it was only a matter of time before she'd have to face the music.

Her heartbeat was fast and uneven and her breathing staggered and panicked. She urged her legs forwards before she changed her mind. As her eyes darted across the faces of her peers, she imagined whispers and judgemental chuckling. She couldn't raise her hands to her ears to block out that loud ringing sound. Her vision was blurring but her locker was in view. Her steps felt heavy as she got closer.

She shoved her face inside of the locker and caught her breath. The ringing and burning stopped and she felt the panic slowly subsiding. As she brushed her hands down her denim skirt to dry them, she shook her head in an effort to control her nerves. Then she took a deep breath.

She'd made a conscious effort that day to look as put together as possible. She was wearing one of her usual cute, stylish and expensive outfits with minimal makeup that left her looking naturally perfect. The blowout she'd given her hair had given it volume without looking as though she'd tried too hard. She only wished she felt as good as she looked.

"Hey, Kendall!" a voice startled her.

Kendall jumped and looked to see where the voice had come from. Daphne stood beside her with a warm smile.

"Hey, Daphne, how are you?" Kendall replied.

"All good. Yourself?"

"Perfect," Kendall lied.

"Could I sit with you at lunch today? It's kind of a long story but I fell out with Jessica who I usually sit with and you seem really nice so I figured I'd ask," Daphne said speedily.

Kendall's heart warmed at the question.

"Of course, I'd love to sit with you. You have great timing actually," Kendall said.

"Great! I'll see you then, bye!" Daphne walked backwards and then headed to class.

Kendall stood smiling at how quickly her day had gotten just a little bit better. She hadn't even thought about who she was going to sit with at lunch, and it occurred to her that if Daphne hadn't asked her, she would've had to sit with her brother.

"*Phew,*" she muttered quietly to herself.

That moment of peace was murdered seconds later when the man who had torn her heart in two and stomped on it, came sauntering down the hallway without a care in the world. To her dismay, he looked as handsome as ever with his rockstar muscles and that Hollywood actor smirk.

She felt actual pain in her chest and had to struggle hard to choke back the urge to cry.

Her mission was to seem completely unfazed by the events of the weekend so that Daniel wouldn't know he had snapped her heart in half.

She didn't want to give him that satisfaction.

Kendall prepared herself for the cruel smirk he would throw her way as he passed, but when it came to it, he walked straight past as if he had never known her at all.

And somehow that hurt more.

***

Kendall had moved back to her usual seat at the front of the classroom so she could be far from Daniel, who would undoubtedly sit at the back.

He swaggered in as if he owned the place and took a seat at the very back. Seated at the front, Kendall didn't have to look at him and she was grateful for that. She wasn't sure if she was imagining the eyes she felt burning a hole in the back of her head.

That first class droned on and so did the rest of them until it was lunchtime.

Kendall's social battery was at an all-time low after being in such close proximity to Daniel all morning but she knew she'd have to perk up in order not to raise any suspicions.

Daphne was already seated and surprisingly Ethan and Austin were with her. She waved Kendall over enthusiastically.

"Hey, little one," her twin greeted as she sat down.

"Hey, Kenny," said Ethan.

"Hi Kendall!" Daphne chirped.

"Hey," she said, trying to match their enthusiasm.

Everyone except Austin, who looked at her sceptically, appeared fooled by her act.

"What's going on with you and Stryker? You guys haven't spoken all day and you've moved away from each other in class?" Ethan asked curiously.

Kendall shrugged, "Just don't really need each other anymore. His grades are up and I got my place at Princeton."

"Wow, you're going to Princeton?! That's amazing!" Daphne said, impressed.

Kendall smiled at her. "Thanks."

Austin looked at her unconvinced, "Are you sure you don't want Ethan and me to have a little *talk* with him?"

Kendall rolled her eyes, "I can handle myself, Aussie."

"Yeah, but you don't have to, when you've got us," Ethan said with a boyish grin.

The remainder of lunch went smoothly, the light conversation taking her mind off of the gigantic void that screamed in agony every time her eyes landed on the brunette boy.

She didn't get up for food - her appetite being rather small of late.

When the warning bell rang she stood and headed to class with Daphne.

They were almost into the hallway when a girl in front of them tripped on her way to the trash can. Her food, spaghetti and chocolate mousse, splattered all over Kendall and to a lesser extent, over Daphne. Kendall felt a throbbing from where the tray had hit her forehead.

When she opened her eyes she saw the cafeteria howling with laughter at the pair of them covered in food.

The horrified girl had fallen to the ground.

"I am so sorry! I tripped. I really didn't mean to do that I swear," she said frantically.

"It's fine," Kendall bit out.

The girl walked away looking extremely embarrassed and a smirking Megan came into view.

Everything clicked into place and Kendall turned red with anger. Megan had obviously tripped the girl, perfectly timed to humiliate her sworn enemies.

"Nice look, Ken," Megan teased and her sheep cackled behind her.

The laughter in the dining hall hadn't died down and Kendall felt nauseous with humiliation. She hated being so out of control of events. She hated that Megan could still make her feel so small.

She couldn't allow her the satisfaction.

"Even when I think you can't get any more pathetic, you still manage to prove me wrong. Points for determination, but this is becoming a bit of an obsession now," Kendall said snidely before grabbing Daphne's hand and barging past Megan, making sure to bump her shoulder so some of the spaghetti sauce transferred onto her.

In the restroom the girls began to clean themselves up. They were more focused on getting it out of their hair and off of their faces as they knew the boys would lend them something to wear.

Kendall felt tears welling up in her eyes, the same tears she had been holding in all day.

They stood in comfortable silence for a few minutes until Kendall's walls crumbled around her and she began to sob uncontrollably.

Chapter 36

An overwhelming wave of emotions consumed Kendall and she couldn't hold back the sobs as she looked at herself in the mirror.

Daphne, alarmed at first by the sudden sobbing, quickly jumped to Kendall's side to give her a hug and stroke her hair.

"It's okay, Kendall. She'll give up eventually. At least we are in this together, right?" Daphne said encouragingly.

Kendall choked back her sobs to respond, "It's not just that."

"What is it?" Daphne asked, concerned.

That question prompted immediate word vomit from Kendall as she began to unload everything that had gone down with Megan, Daniel, and her mother over the past few weeks.

Daphne stood there shocked for a moment as she processed all of the news she had just heard.

"H- how did Megan even know I was allergic to bees?" Daphne asked, looking nervous.

Kendall shrugged, "She always has her ways."

Daphne huffed and gave Kendall another comforting hug.

"I'm so sorry Daniel treated you like that. You don't deserve it and believe me when I say it says way more about him than it does about you," Daphne said into Kendall's shoulder.

Kendall sniffed, "Thanks Daphne. You're a really good person."

They separated to smile at each other.

"So are you," Daphne said assuredly.

They spent the rest of lunch in the girl's bathroom just venting and giving each other advice as they picked spaghetti out of their hair.

Kendall was grateful for the opportunity to tell someone what had happened. She was hesitant to tell Chris knowing how close she and Daniel were. She didn't want Chris to feel in the middle of anything, so she chose to keep it from her for a while. Daphne offered her some helpful encouragement and advice and Kendall knew this wouldn't be the last time they'd be recovering from a Megan prank together.

Ethan gave her a hoodie to cover her stained clothes and Austin did the same for Daphne. Kendall loved seeing the two of them together. They were like love sick puppies, even though they were in complete denial about their feelings for each other.

The rest of the school day was uneventful and painful, with three classes left to endure with Daniel. Finally, the school day ended and she made it home and fled to her room to hibernate until the following morning.

Her mother had left for a spa retreat when Kendall returned from Daniel's house a broken mess that Sunday night and no one knew when she would return.

Kendall enjoyed the silent house.

***

Days began to blend together.

She went to school and acted like she didn't notice Daniel's presence or smell his cologne as he walked past her in the halls. She swallowed the bile in her throat and fought back tears as she did so. She sat with Daphne, Ethan, Austin and occasionally some of the other football guys at lunch. Every day she endured some kind of Megan torture, then recovered from it in the restrooms with Daphne. She dragged herself through the final classes of the day, went to volleyball practice and then home to sleep the remainder of the day away.

She was unhappy.

Surrounded as she was by so many people who cared about her, she had never felt so alone.

Halloween had rolled around and Kendall could not have been more excited. She was more than ready to drink the night away at a party in a playboy bunny costume and make questionable decisions.

Chris had invited her and Daphne to a party and they had already been shopping together for their costumes.

Kendall strutted into the party with the most confidence she had felt since Daniel had torn her heart from her body many moons ago. The confidence may have had something to do with the alcohol already running through her system from the pre-gaming they'd done whilst getting dolled up at Daphne's house.

Each wore a latex body suit that left little to the imagination from the back, bunny ears, sheer black tights, black heels, a bunny tail, and pretty much nothing else.

Kendall was relieved she had gotten ready at Daphne's house since Austin would've flipped out if he saw her leaving the house dressed like that. Kendall knew he was bound to be in attendance at the party but he wouldn't be able to do much when she was already there.

Wolf whistles and judgemental whispers followed her as she made her way to the kitchen without a care in the world.

"Shots?" Kendall asked, looking at Daphne and Chris who were completely on board.

They wasted no time in pouring vodka into red plastic shot cups and tossing them back in unison.

The burning liquid travelled down Kendall's throat and she fought the urge to wince.

"Hey Kendall, I haven't seen you in ages," Kai's voice interrupted their shot fest.

Kendall turned to face him and tried her best to smile, "Hey."

He looked at her sceptically, suddenly clocking her obvious hesitancy towards him. "Before you say anything... I have no idea what went down with you and Dan. But whatever it was, I had nothing to do with it. I hope you guys can work it out, but regardless, I'd still really like to be your friend."

She hadn't known that was exactly what she wanted to hear, but when he said it, it was like music to her ears. She smiled genuinely and gave him a tight hug.

"Take some shots with us!" Chris yelled, and they all cheered before pouring another round and knocking them back instantly.

Four shots later and Kendall was giddier than she had felt in a long while. They all sang loudly to the music as they poured more shots and Kendall swayed her hips sensually to the beat.

"Hey gorgeous," a deep voice said into her ear as large hands gently grabbed her hips.

On any other day Kendall would have elbowed the handsy horn dog for touching her without asking, but there was too much vodka and vengeance running through her veins.

The thought of another guy giving her the right amount of attention after she'd been feeling so terrible about herself all week, was far too exciting to turn down.

She swivelled round and came face to face with a smirking Luke.

Again, on any other day she would snap at him to get off, but on this day, she finally noticed how handsome he was and how nice it felt to have his big hands on her body.

That was enough for her.

"Want to play never have I ever?" Kendall asked, smirking.

Chapter 37

With ungodly amounts of alcohol coursing through her veins, Kendall was very much an open book and very much unopposed to Luke's hands being all over her.

Around ten or twelve people were leaning against the kitchen island ready to play the game. Daphne had disappeared, undoubtedly to go and find Austin.

Luke was behind Kendall with his entire front pressed up against her back and his hands roaming everywhere they could. She didn't mind. The attention was feeding her alcohol inflated ego.

"Never have I ever... faked an orgasm," a girl said, causing every girl in the circle to immediately take a shot, except Kendall.

Everyone looked at her sceptically.

"What? I haven't," she said defensively.

"Oh wait, I forgot. You're a virgin!" one of the sheep in the circle said, laughing loudly.

Kendall hadn't even known there was a sheep amongst them until she heard her howling like a hyena.

Others in the circle began laughing but Kendall's confidence didn't falter.

"Actually, that's not true. Not that there would've been anything wrong with it if I was. You're just jealous because you've probably never even had an orgasm that didn't come from something made of silicone," Kendall said.

The sheep's cackling subsided and the rest of the circle smirked at Kendall's comeback.

The game resumed and Kendall was becoming more and more legless by the minute. It came to the point where Luke's arms were practically holding her up.

"Come on, let's go sit down somewhere," he whispered into her ear and dragged her like a rag doll over to the sofas in the living room. He placed her onto his lap so that she was straddling him.

Chris noticed the interaction and went to find Blake so the pair of them could spy on Kendall and Luke inconspicuously. She found him outside smoking with Kai and Daniel no less.

"Come on, we have an undercover task," Chris said, taking Blake's hand and attempting to pull him out of his seat.

"What task?" he said, uninterested.

"We need to spy on my friend to make sure she doesn't do anything stupid or get taken advantage of. Now come," Chris said adamantly.

Daniel piped up, "You don't have any girlfriends. Unless..."

Realisation hit him.

"Kendall?" he said, putting the pieces together.

Chris scoffed like it was a ridiculous guess.

"She's getting taken advantage of?" he growled agitatedly.

"Shut up, what do you care? You kicked her ass to the curb and now suddenly you're worried about her well-being?" Chris spat.

Daniel huffed, "It's complicated."

"Sounds pretty damn simple to me, Stryker," Chris said, finally successfully pulling Blake up from his seat and dragging him inside.

Meanwhile in the living room, Luke had latched his lips onto Kendall's neck whilst she seemed to be slipping in and out of consciousness.

Kendall's mind was completely absent and she was totally unaware of what she was doing. Luke however, was very much aware, as he used his hands on Kendall's hips to grind her against him.

Chris and Blake gasped at the sight but before either of them could do a thing, Kendall was torn from Luke's lips by someone else. Daniel was suddenly in view, pulling Luke up by his collar and slammed his body to the ground. Punch after punch landed at Luke's face until Kai and Blake, with great difficulty, pulled Daniel off. Luke scrambled to his feet and fled the scene.

Daniel was breathing heavily with murder in his eyes.

Chris scanned the room to see where Kendall had gotten to, only to find her curled up in a ball on the floor by the stairs with her ears plugged.

She ran over to her friend and pried her hands away from her ears, lifting her head to look at her.

"Are you okay?" Chris asked, concerned.

Kendall's eyes were droopy and she looked ready to crash. Daniel rushed to Chris' side.

"Is she okay?" he said frantically.

"She's blackout drunk. So yes, she's right as rain," Chris said sarcastically.

Austin appeared suddenly.

"Where is she?!" he yelled and scanned the room furiously.

"Lockwood!" Chris yelled to get his attention and began lifting Kendall's limp body from the ground.

"Why the fuck is my sister dressed like a hooker?" he spat.

"It's Halloween dude," Chris said.

"Let me drive her home," Daniel offered.

Austin's eyes darkened, "You can stay the fuck away from her. I don't know what happened with you two but I gave you simple orders not to hurt her. Watch your back, Stryker."

"You don't know what went down," Daniel spat.

"She's black out drunk in a playboy bunny costume and she was just found in the arms of someone she usually hates. And all suspiciously after the two of you ended whatever alliance you had going on. I don't have time for your bullshit excuses," Austin said venomously.

"He's got a point," Chris chimed in.

Austin huffed as he tried to think of a way to get Kendall safely to bed. He had been drinking so he couldn't drive, there were no taxis in that particular area past 2am, and he couldn't walk her home yet.

"Hey listen, I know the guy who owns this house. I can take her upstairs to one of the guest rooms and stay with her all night, then walk her back home tomorrow morning," Chris said.

Austin looked sceptical, but she did seem trustworthy and it was no doubt the best option they had at that moment in time.

"Fine. I'll come up and check on her before I leave. Thank you," Austin agreed.

***

After spewing her guts up, getting showered off by Chris, brushing her teeth, and getting into someone's sweatpants and T-shirt, Kendall was tucked up in bed with Chris on her phone beside her.

There was a knock on the door. Austin had already come to check on her so Chris was confused as to who it might be. She opened the door just a crack to see the intruder.

Daniel stood before her looking extremely stressed and uneasy.

"Is she okay? Can I see her?" he asked.

Chapter 38

"You've got five minutes with her and that's it. I'm only letting you talk to her because I know damn well she isn't going to remember a thing you say," Chris said sassily, and walked out of the guest bedroom.

That left Daniel and Kendall alone.

"Who's there?" Kendall said dazedly, as she lay on the bed staring at the ceiling.

Daniel stepped further into the room and took a seat on the edge of the bed. He faced away from her and stared at the wall intently.

"Are you okay?" he asked softly.

There was movement behind him, as she sat up.

"Like you care," she said childishly.

"Did he hurt you?" Daniel asked, ignoring her obvious distaste for him.

"That's hilarious coming from you."

"Damn it Kendall, just tell me you're okay," he said, raising his voice.

"I'm not!" she snapped.

Daniel's gaze softened.

She swayed slightly from the alcohol that was still doing wonders to her physical and mental state.

"And I'm not sure why you're suddenly acting like you care when you are the reason I'm not doing well," she countered.

He looked down guiltily.

"You played me, you lied to me, and you smirked in my face at the same time," she said weakly.

She lay back down and pulled the covers up to her chin, "Go back to the party, Daniel."

He felt a sting in his chest as she said his name.

"Princess, please," he pleaded.

He was met with nothing but heavy breathing as Kendall fell into a deep sleep.

He sighed, "In a few years you'll be graduating from Princeton at the top of your class and I will just be an insignificant figure from your past. I will smile as I watch you succeed and achieve everything in life that you deserve. I will hold on to our memories so you can move on and forget all about them. I hate that I never told you. There is so much more I wish I could have said before our time was up. I'm sorry I had to hurt you."

There was a silent pause before the door opened and Chris sauntered in.

"Time's up, Stryker."

***

Life went on. It wasn't the same, but it went on.

The torture from Megan continued as expected. Daniel went back to pretending Kendall didn't exist and Kendall went back to pretending she didn't feel her heartstrings snap every time he walked past her in the halls without so much as a glance.

Mrs Lockwood continued making passive aggressive remarks to Kendall. Ethan was her number one guy once more, and they went back to regularly hanging out.

She battled daily to find a new normal after being so fond of the old one. She hadn't realised how happy Daniel had made her until he was nowhere to be seen.

It was hard struggling to unlove someone whom she had never admitted she was in love with in the first place.

Irony can be so painful.

Weeks turned into months and suddenly it was January fifth, the first day back at school after winter break.

Kendall sashayed into school with Daphne beside her and Ethan and her twin brother trailing behind.

Her confident facade was the only thing keeping her from falling apart.

The day was as normal and as boring as any regular day of high school, until gym class rolled around in the second till last period.

Dodgeball was the domain of the popular kids. It was nothing more than an opportunity for the lazy gym teachers to sit on their backsides whilst the highest members of the school's hierarchy launched balls at those lower than them.

No remorse, no regard for the rules or people's feelings. Not a single care in the world.

Kendall was good at sports so this game never scared her. In fact, she was pretty damn good at it. However, she had not been prepared for the turn of events that took place in the gym that afternoon.

The teams were mixed boys and girls. Kendall's absolutely stellar good luck landed her on the opposite team to Megan and the sheep, and Daniel no less.

This didn't frighten her in the slightest but turned out not to be in her favour later on in the game.

With no real effort, Kendall played along with Daphne at her side and paid no attention to the success (or lack thereof) of her team that was losing horribly.

Kendall crouched to grab a ball only to realise there were no dodge-balls on her side of the line.

She looked up to see Megan, the sheep, and some random popular kid wannabes, holding all the dodgeballs with menacing looks on their faces.

Megan looked so excited she seemed fit to spontaneously combust.

Suddenly, fifteen rubber dodgeballs came hurtling towards Kendall. She was completely defenceless as they all hit her simultaneously.

Pain seared through her as the harsh smack of rubber impacted her skin.

Laughter erupted throughout the gym as Kendall looked up to see Megan looking even more smug than ever.

Kendall's blood boiled and adrenaline took over from the pain in her body.

She stormed furiously towards Megan, who grew increasingly hesitant with every step.

Using all her strength, Kendall reached the blonde girl and putting her hands on Megan's shoulders, she shoved her to the ground. Megan, gasping in surprise, fell painfully onto her back.

The crowd gasped as Kendall straddled Megan's waist and slammed her fist into Megan's petrified face.

Kendall, ignoring the pain in her knuckles, glared down at the pathetic girl beneath her.

"I warned you not to make this a physical fight, Megan. Big mistake on your part," Kendall spat venomously.

The girls looked horrified, whilst the guys looked a cross between impressed and amused.

The lazy gym teacher trudged over to whisk her away to the principal's office. But even that wasn't enough to wipe the triumphant smirk off Kendall's face as she stared down at Megan clutching her bleeding nose.

Chapter 39

Kendall sat in the principal's office with a million different concerns circling her mind.

Although the punch felt good in the moment, it left her with bruised knuckles and punishable consequences.

"I don't understand how this has happened, Miss Lockwood. You are not a violent individual," the principal said, sounding disappointed.

Kendall sighed, "Megan has been torturing me for months now with pranks and constant humiliation on a daily basis and everyone seemed to turn a blind eye to it. I've finally had enough."

"Harmless pranks should not be avenged with acts of violence," the women said harshly. "Megan could have a broken nose because of you,"

Kendall knew she should feel guilty but she didn't. Regardless of the inevitable punishment, she couldn't stop the anger inside of her from boiling over.

"It's not my fault Megan picked a fight she couldn't win," Kendall spat.

The principal's eyes widened disapprovingly.

Kendall took a deep agitated breath before elaborating, "With all due respect Miss, those 'harmless pranks' you seem so eager to brush under the rug, are actually acts of bullying. I'm sick of being told to just grin and bear it and then being scolded for sticking up for myself. I'm not a violent person by any means, but I can't promise this won't happen again unless Megan leaves me completely alone."

The wrinkled woman was at a loss for words. She nudged her spectacles further up her nose and straightened her mouth into a tight line.

"Head back to class, Miss Lockwood. Send Mr Stryker in on your way out," she said and began shifting things around her desk.

Even hearing his name made Kendall's body rigid and alert.

She nodded and headed out of the office. She had prepared herself to see him when she opened the door, but nothing could have prepared her for the state he was in.

Hunched over in a chair with his forearms resting on his thighs, he was tapping his foot. More concerning was the torn-up state of his knuckles along with the sizable bruise on his cheek and the dried blood on his busted lip.

He looked up when he heard her enter and she held back a gasp at his beaten up state. Thirty minutes ago he'd been bruise-free, so Kendall was beyond curious as to know what had happened in such a short space of time.

"What happened to you?" she asked before she could stop herself.

He chuckled, "You're not the only one running around punching people today."

Kendall's chest tightened at the mere sound of his voice. A small part of her wished seeing him so hurt would make her feel good.

It didn't.

"Who's the other guy?" she asked.

"More than one guy but it doesn't really matter now. Won't be a problem again," he said dismissively.

"Right," she said shyly.

He stared at her for a minute. She wasn't sure if she was imagining it but she could've sworn he was looking at her the same way he used to.

Like he was admiring her or studying her, or both.

She was conflicted between wanting the look in his eyes to vanish and wanting him to never look away.

"You were pretty badass in gym. Didn't know you had it in you," he said smiling slightly.

Kendall offered a lopsided smile as she tried not to overthink every word he said.

"The principal asked me to send you in," Kendall said simply and headed to class without looking back.

Daniel watched her walk away with that same longing look in his eyes.

***

"I cannot believe I missed the best cat fight of the year," Ethan whined from the passenger seat.

"Shut up. It was hardly a cat fight," Kendall said, as she drove them home from school.

"You broke her nose! I would've very much enjoyed seeing that," Ethan said enthusiastically.

Kendall shrugged and then remembered something.

"Hey wait, do you know why Daniel was in the principal's office looking like he got into a fight with a grizzly bear," she asked.

"Oh yeah, I was gonna ask you about that. What happened between you two because I thought I had it figured out and then today happened and now I'm confused," Ethan said frantically.

Kendall's eyebrows knitted together in confusion, "What happened today that confused you? And you still haven't answered my question."

"Well Dan got into a fight in the locker room with like, half the basketball team because they were talking about you. That's what I heard at least," Ethan said nonchalantly.

"Wait what?!" Kendall said.

"I know right. Apparently, he put up a pretty good fight even though he was way too outnumbered," Ethan added.

"What did they say about me?" Kendall asked, even more confused.

"Well, from what I've been told, they were just being all pervy about you straddling Megan. Just making something out of nothing. Daniel just lost it and punched their lights out. I probably would've done the same."

Kendall's eyes widened and her brain spun as she tried to register everything he said.

"I don't get it. That doesn't seem like something you would do if you don't care about someone," she said, more to herself than to Ethan.

"That's because he obviously *does* still care about you. He stares at you all the time when you're not looking and he threatens any guy that talks about you. I really just wish you'd tell me what happened between you two," Ethan said.

Her heart lifted slightly.

"Why have you never told me any of that before?" she said, annoyed.

"Every time I say his name you give me that death glare like you're gonna kick me in the balls if I continue," Ethan said defensively.

"He stares at me?" Kendall asked.

"All the time," Ethan said.

"And threatens guys who talk about me?" she added.

"Regularly," he replied.

Kendall stared straight ahead and shook her head in disbelief.

"I don't understand this."

***

The following day was one that Kendall wasn't sure was actually real.

Everything was routine and ordinary until lunch time.

Kendall strolled down the hallway towards the cafeteria with Daphne at her side.

Before they made it to the entrance however, a certain blonde came into view and denied them access.

Megan stood before them, looking less than perfect thanks to the bandage covering her nose. Her stance was less demanding than usual and much more unsure.

Kendall huffed, "Get out of my way, Megan."

Megan smiled sheepishly, "I was actually hoping I could talk to you both."

Daphne scoffed.

"No thank you," Kendall said, attempting to sidestep Megan.

Megan moved with her, blocking her path.

"Please, It will only take a minute," she pleaded.

Kendall rolled her eyes and Daphne looked down nervously.

"Fine. Talk," Kendall said.

Passing students were looking interested. Some even stopped to watch what would unfold. Daniel and Austin also paused in their tracks.

Megan looked around worriedly, "Can we go somewhere more private?"

Kendall folded her arms, "Not a chance. I would like to keep the witnesses. Now *talk*."

Daphne kept her eyes down, trying to ignore the watching eyes. Confrontation was never really her thing.

Megan took a deep breath.

"I'm sorry. I was cruel to both of you and it was unfair and unjust. I hope you can forgive me," Megan said as she held her head high to hide her embarrassment.

The hallway fell silent as the surrounding students awaited Kendall's reply.

Kendall stayed looking bored, whilst Daphne looked shocked.

Kendall giggled humourlessly, "Right. Okay, Megan."

Megan looked deflated slightly and her smile weakened.

Kendall rolled her eyes and, taking Daphne's wrist, steered her around Megan and into the cafeteria.

Megan didn't move from the spot as student's giggled and whispered around her. They filtered out of the hallway slowly and left the blonde girl staring hopelessly at the ground.

Soon enough, after her humiliation had sunk in, Megan took a shaky breath and slowly made her way towards the exit. She flung the doors open and kept walking as the winter air chilled her skin. She hopped inside her BMW Mini to escape the cold. Her hands reached forward to switch on the ignition and she backed up out of her parking space and made her way onto the main road.

Once she was completely out of the school's view, she burst into tears.

Chapter 40

Kendall had found Megan's apology to be obnoxious and ill-intentioned, but she couldn't help feeling guilty about how she had responded.

Her pride had spoken for her.

Kendall had long fantasised about humiliating Megan in front of everyone, just as Megan and the sheep had humiliated her. Not only from senior year, but for most of their friendship.

But when it came down to it, watching Megan fight the urge to cry did not bring Kendall any joy.

A week had gone by and Megan had been absent since she walked out of school following the incident.

The fall of Megan Saunders as the school's queen bee had created all kinds of buzz that was yet to die down.

"I still can't figure out if she was being serious or not," Daphne said, poking mindlessly at her salad.

Ethan spoke up, "I hate to be the one to say it, but I think she was."

Kendall, Daphne and Austin turned to look at him critically.

"You do?" Kendall raised an eyebrow.

"Her friends hung her out to dry after she got a busted nose and didn't look perfect anymore. It's not crazy to think that maybe she thought she could start giving out olive branches instead of burning bridges. It isn't like she had anything to lose. Maybe she thought years of friendship with Kendall counted for something," Ethan said.

Every eye on the table was sceptical but Kendall's were particularly ominous.

"Are you seriously suggesting I'm the bad guy here for not forgiving her?" Kendall asked incredulously.

Ethan huffed, "That's not what I said."

Kendall rolled her eyes and stood up, "You didn't have to say it. I know that's what you meant."

Ethan opened his mouth to interject but Kendall was already storming off.

Austin's mouth became a tight line and his eyebrows raised. Daphne went back to poking her salad. Ethan huffed agitatedly and rested his chin in his hand.

"Women," he muttered grumpily.

***

Later that day, Kendall was handed a pink detention slip by the teacher from her fifth period class. She tried to dispute it but the old man assured her he had no idea what it was for and she should talk to whoever was running detention that day.

Kendall had never had detention. Ever.

Through gritted teeth, she nodded and completed the class before furiously stomping down the hallway. Once at the classroom listed on the pink slip, her eyebrows furrowed at the sight of who else was there.

Megan was sitting at the teacher's desk with an even better nose than the one that had been broken. Kendall took a step back at the mischievous look in Megan's face. The only other person in the room was Daniel Stryker, looking as bored as on the first day of senior year in the principal's office.

Kendall took another step backwards at the sight. But before she could escape, she heard the sound of a lock and saw Ethan's guilty face through the glass window of the door.

Her heart sank.

"Do come and take a seat, Kendall, detention is now in session," Megan said, a suspicious amount of joy in her voice.

Kendall turned back, "What the hell is going on? How did you manage to give me a real detention slip?"

"I was wondering the same thing," Daniel piped up.

At the sound of his husky voice, Kendall's brain went into a spin.

Megan clasped her hands together on the desk in front of her.

"That's unimportant, but if you must know, I frequently abuse my power as student body president," Megan said nonchalantly.

Kendall chuckled.

"*You don't say*," she muttered.

Megan gestured to the seat beside Daniel, "Please, sit."

Kendall's eyes narrowed, "Woof."

Daniel chuckled from his seat.

Megan's persistence seemed to know no bounds, "You will be in this room for as long as it takes to address my agenda and I will not begin explaining that agenda until you are seated."

Kendall huffed but complied, reluctantly taking a seat beside Daniel.

Daniel's eyes lingered on her for a moment too long and Kendall met his gaze. They both whipped their heads back to face the front where Megan was grinning.

She took a deep breath as she stood from the teacher's desk and stared down at the pair.

"As you may know, the past week has not been my finest. I was punched, stitched and puffy in the face. I was then shunned, humiliated and bedridden due to my colossal drop in popularity. I lost all of my minions and turned to my last hope; the only real friend I've ever known, Kendall Lockwood," Megan paused for effect.

Kendall felt a pang of guilt.

"But alas, the damage was irreparable. During my hibernation, I found strength in my struggle. I decided that you cannot be an icon without scandal and that bouncing back would only make people love me more."

Kendall rolled her eyes and Daniel sighed.

"What does this have to do with us?" Daniel asked impatiently.

Megan smiled, "I'm glad you asked.

"I spent a lot of time at home over the past week, which I usually avoid doing for a multitude of reasons. The main reason being my mother is always there and she often has her annoying friends over for wine and cheese. However, during all the time spent at home, I uncovered a scandal much larger than my dethroning. And it involves the two of you."

Kendall and Daniel looked confused.

Kendall spoke up, "Megan, if this is all some practical joke to get back at me for what happened in the hall-"

"It's not," Megan interrupted.

Kendall felt relieved.

"I may have been reinstated as queen bee and my minions may be back in full force but I apologised to you last week because I meant it. It hurt me that you blew me off, but I am aware now that I didn't deserve your forgiveness. I don't know if I deserve it at all, but after you've seen what I am about to show you, I hope you will at least believe in my sincerity," Megan said and clicked the play button on her phone.

Daniel looked over at Kendall anxiously.

Mrs Lockwood's muffled voice came through the phone.

"I know it sounds harsh. I know, I know. But I had to teach the little brat a lesson. The boy made it all too easy for me. If they were as close as my daughter claimed they were, that boy would have known that Kendall has absolutely no interest in her father's whereabouts,"

Other women were heard chuckling in response.

Kendall's eyebrows knitted as Daniel squeezed his eyes shut.

"Oh Miriam, don't look at me like that. You would do the same, if your children weren't far too young for you to threaten to cut them off financially. Honestly, It's the best thing I've ever done. They haven't seen each other since."

The recording ended and the room was silent.

Daniel was pinching the bridge of his nose, looking frustrated, whilst Kendall looked as though she had just seen a ghost.

Megan spoke up first, "As you may have heard, that was Kendall's mother explaining a rather conniving plan to her friends at my house. You guys stopped hanging out quite abruptly and I always wondered why. You should probably talk about this. Ethan and I will be outside in the hall and we are not letting you leave until you have sorted things out."

She walked to the door and slipped out, locking it behind her before either of them could protest.

Chapter 41

There was a long silence.

Kendall slowly turned her head to face Daniel.

"I knew it," she said, barely above a whisper.

Daniel didn't look at her.

"My mother made you? How could I have not thought of that? Of course, she would be behind all this," Kendall said, more to herself than to Daniel.

"You weren't supposed to find out," Daniel finally spoke.

Kendall felt lost, "I don't understand. Why didn't you just tell me? We could have figured something out."

He finally lifted his head but faced forwards, "It wasn't that simple. I had no choice."

"Explain it to me."

Daniel's jaw clenched. No response.

Kendall grew impatient, "Daniel, the jig is up!"

As he turned his head, she met his sad gaze.

He sighed before diving into the phone call he had received from Mrs Lockwood the day after the wedding. He spared no details.

Everything fell into place and Kendall had a sudden urge to throw up.

She had never expected her mother to stoop so low and she felt the sharp pang of betrayal in her chest.

"Daniel, I hate to break it to you, but my mother lied to you," Kendall said.

He raised an eyebrow, urging her to continue.

Kendall nodded weakly and looking straight ahead, told him, "I got a full academic scholarship to Princeton. In addition to that, my Grandparents set me up with a trust fund that I received on my eighteenth birthday so I am financially independent. There is nothing my mother could have done to stop me from going to college."

Daniel sighed and dropped his head into his hands.

"Are you serious?" he mumbled.

"As a heart attack."

He raised his head but his eyes remained scrunched closed.

"You may have also heard on that recording that I have no interest in knowing about my dad," Kendall said sheepishly.

Daniel huffed before chuckling humourlessly as he shook his head in disbelief.

"So, you're telling me this has all been for nothing?" he said, sounding defeated.

Kendall nodded slowly, "Yeah."

Daniel opened his eyes and looked over at her. He was smiling with sad eyes.

"Why did you never tell me you got a full ride?" Daniel asked.

She shrugged awkwardly, "I didn't want to make you feel bad. You were still struggling in class and I was worried it might seem like I was bragging."

Daniel chuckled, "You have got to be kidding me."

"I realise now how stupid that sounds," Kendall said guiltily.

He shook his head and slowly stood up.

"I was the stupid one. I should have come to you with the problem. I was just so worried your future would be ruined if I was selfish enough to want to keep you. I knew you would've gotten over me eventually," Daniel said, looking down at her.

She stood up from the desk and walked around it to meet him.

He took her hand into his and stroked it with his thumb.

She smiled and shook her head, "I don't know if I would have ever gotten over you."

Daniel's face broke out into his signature smirk, "I am pretty unforgettable."

Kendall scoffed, "Ugh, shut up, Stryker."

He raised her hand to his lips and gave it a chaste kiss.

"Come on, *Princess*, don't be like that," he cooed.

She smiled remembering the first day of school in the Principal's office when he first said those exact words.

"Can I kiss you?" he asked quietly.

Kendall smiled and leaned in, "You better."

He met her in the middle and placed his soft lips on hers. They both smiled into the kiss and moved their bodies closer. Kendal clasped her arms around the nape of his neck whilst Daniel's hands touched her waist to pull her in close.

Kendall's skin felt on fire where his hands touched her and her brain was spinning.

His lips moved passionately against hers as though he couldn't get enough of her, and she savoured every second of it.

Their bodies were impossibly close and they seemed to fit together like puzzle pieces.

They pulled apart to rest their foreheads against each other, needing to catch their breath.

"I've missed you, Princess," he said huskily.

She couldn't fight the childish smile that broke out on her face.

"I've missed you too."

They took a moment to get lost in each other's eyes.

"I think I kinda love you," Daniel said breathlessly, before he could stop himself.

Kendall felt the world around her disappear as she looked into his captivating blue eyes.

That was all she had wanted to hear.

All she ever needed to hear ever again.

"I love you too."

Chapter 42

It took a while for them to fully convince Ethan and Megan they had made up so they could be granted freedom from the classroom. They were practically reciting vows just to prove they were back together.

At last the door was unlocked and Kendall felt an overwhelming gratitude towards Megan. So much so that she enveloped her in a hug without even thinking.

The hug took Megan by surprise but she gave in to the warm embrace, laughing softly.

Ethan directed Daniel down the hallway to give the girls a moment of privacy.

"Thank you, Megan," Kendall said tearfully into her blonde hair.

"Does this mean I'm forgiven?"

Kendall pulled away to smile at her former best friend, "You are forgiven."

"Then I should be the one thanking you," Megan said with a sad smile.

Kendall looked unsure how to respond.

"I'm mad at myself for screwing up the only real friendship I've ever known," Megan said.

Kendall shook her head, ready to provide reassurance, but Megan continued before she had a chance.

"I know it was corrupt and exhausting at times but for the first couple of years it was the only thing in my life that mattered to me.

"I know I changed and it suddenly seemed like I cared more about boys and popularity than you, but the truth is that I was just so incredibly jealous of you, Kendall."

Kendall's eyes widened.

She could not, even for a second, imagine Megan being jealous of her. Let alone fathom out why.

Megan was perfect and everyone knew it. Kendall couldn't imagine what she might have, that Megan would be envious of.

"Don't look so surprised, Kendall. You're the kind of girl that guys write songs about. And you're like a butterfly because you are so oblivious to just how beautiful you are. Standing next to you made me feel like a troll sometimes.

"You're probably the only person who I will ever admit that to," Megan chuckled.

There was a thoughtful pause as Kendall wondered how on earth someone as stunning as Megan could ever feel like a *troll*.

"I shouldn't have projected my insecurities onto you to make you feel small when I knew you already had your mother doing that to you at home. I was childish and immature but I am trying to be better than that now.

"It's a working progress but I am going to need to get off my high horse if I have any hope of climbing the social food chain in Alabama," Megan said.

Kendall's face lit up in surprise, "You got into Alabama?! Oh my goodness, congratulations!"

Megan couldn't fight her excited grin, "Thank you! And congratulations on your full ride to Princeton."

"Thank you!" Kendall chuckled giddily.

Megan nodded.

"For everything," Kendall added before shifting her weight to start walking towards Daniel down the hall.

Megan sighed and gave her an appreciative smile.

Kendall quickly remembered something and began walking backwards, adding as she did so, "Oh, and about climbing the social food chain at Alabama,"

She paused to smirk, "give 'em hell."

Megan chuckled and shook her head as she watched Kendall's retreating figure.

Chapter 43

A ustin was speechless after hearing the recording of his mother's cruel plan. Kendall wasn't exactly sure why though, as she
didn't see it as remotely out of character for Mrs Lockwood.

"I actually can't believe she went this far," he said, looking down
with scrunched eyebrows.

"I can." Kendall stated.

He looked at his sister, "We have to do something. There's no way
we can continue to live with that witch."

"I'm so glad you feel that way..." Kendall smiled mischievously.
"Because I called Grandma and we have a plan."

***

The plan fell into place a mere 24 hours later when Mrs Lockwood
came home from work with her usual snobby attitude.

Austin and Kendall were standing expectantly in the foyer as
movers were pottering about with boxes.

Mrs Lockwood could be heard screeching from the driveway before the front door was even open. The movers ignored her commands and instead pretended they couldn't hear her at all.

The double doors were flung open and a dishevelled Mrs Lockwood stomped in.

"What is the meaning of this!" she bellowed.

Kendall couldn't help the smile that crept onto her face, "You're moving out."

"Yes, *mother*," Austin patronised.

She squinted furiously, "I beg your pardon!"

"You heard them," a voice sounded from up on the landing.

Mrs Lockwood visibly stiffened as her eyes darted to her own mother descending the stairs.

"Mother," she gulped.

Kendall's smirk widened as her plan unfolded seamlessly before her.

"Allow me to explain," the older lady said.

She coughed to clear her throat and went on,

"It has come to my attention that you have been making my grandbabies unhappy. You've been degrading and controlling them for your own selfish reasons, just like you have done to everyone in your life since you were a child."

Mrs Lockwood's eyes were fearful as her mother continued,

"You crossed the line this time, darling, so I'm taking back the house and giving it to them. What they choose to do with it is up to them. I gave this house to you to raise a family. This is not a family."

Kendall watched her mother sink to the ground and smack a hand over her mouth, trying to muffle her painful sobbing. Grandma's expression gave nothing away.

Mrs Lockwood was a trembling mess at her mother's feet and the twins looked at each other guiltily.

But before their good natures prompted them to abort the plan, Grandma spoke again, "Don't let this act fool you, kids. She got fake crying down to an art before she even said her first words."

Mrs Lockwood's cries dried up as though a switch had been flipped and Kendall no longer felt any remorse.

"How could you do this to your own child?" Mrs Lockwood asked helplessly.

Her mother squinted at her, "I could ask you the same thing."

Mrs Lockwood looked down shamefacedly. Seemingly with nothing left to say.

"You have plenty of properties of your own and you have enough money to last a lifetime, so don't be drama queen and act like we are subjecting you to a life on the streets," their grandma said finally.

Kendall took that as an opportunity to step forwards and say her final words, "I'd like you to leave my house now."

Her mother looked over at her indignantly.

She didn't even have it in her to utter one last evil remark; she simply whipped her head around and marched out of the front door, slamming it behind her.

Austin and Kendall each released a breath they hadn't realised they were holding, and smiled excitedly at each other.

Kendall wrapped her brother in an embrace and their grandma came over to join in.

"Thank you for doing that for us, Grandma," Kendall said, enjoying the warm sets of arms squeezing her tight.

The older lady chuckled softly, "No one hurts my babies, not even my other baby."

They stayed like that until the movers had taken all Mrs Lockwood's belongings.

Finally, after some family bonding and catching up, they bid their grandma farewell. The moment the door clicked shut the twins looked at each other with the same mischievous look.

"Party?" Austin asked.

Kendall nodded.

"Party."

Epilogue

Kendall leisurely placed her books into her locker and gasped when a large arm snaked around her waist.

Recognising Daniel's masculine scent, she blushed as he nuzzled his face into her neck.

"Someone missed me over the weekend," Kendall said, teasingly.

Daniel scoffed and spun her round to face him. In one fluid motion he pinned her up against the lockers, his arms caging her in.

His cocky smirk sparkled down at her and she couldn't fight the smile tugging at her lips.

"I didn't miss you. Why? Did you miss *me*?" Daniel said playfully, leaning closer.

Kendall faked a grimace, "Miss you? What is there to miss?"

Daniel rolled his eyes before capturing her mouth with his. The kiss started off competitive and rough, becoming slow and passionate, as usual.

"Rake in the PDA guys. I shouldn't be exposed to this graphic behaviour, I'm just a boy," Kai's voice interrupted their heavy make out session.

They broke apart and saw him, his face painted with disgrace and a hand over his heart.

Kendall chuckled at Kai's hilarious greeting, but Daniel looked less than pleased at the intrusion.

"Shut up, Kai. I've walked in on you balls deep in random women an unbelievable number of times. I think you can handle seeing us kissing," Daniel said firmly.

Kai grinned like a child, "I'm going to choose to ignore that accusation and focus on the real situation at hand."

Kendall and Daniel blinked at him.

"You guys are finally together!" Kai sang and wrapped his arms around the pair of them.

Daniel stood still, waiting for the embrace to end, whilst Kendall snuggled into Kai's side.

"That's enough of that, time for class," Daniel said in a clipped tone.

Kendall rolled her eyes at her boyfriend and they walked off together down the hallway.

Kai gasped, "Danny boy is concerned about his punctuality in school?! What have you done to him, Ken-doll?!"

Kendall chuckled at the new nickname and they headed to class with not a care in the world.

***

Saturday nights meant one thing for Kendall these days... fight club.

Or at least that's what she called it.

Daniel had told her numerous times not to call it that because it made it sound '*Lame*'.

Predictably, Kendall did not care. She found it fitting and argued that he should take it as a compliment because Tyler Durdin was hot.

Regardless, Saturday nights were spent at Circuit- or rather they were spent underneath Circuit.

Daniel won every week but always came out of the ring battered and bloody, a sight Kendall found surprisingly sexy.

This Saturday was Daniel's first fight where Kendall, as his girl-friend, actually had permission to attend. Kendall was waiting anxiously by the ring with crossed fingers whilst Chris and Blake bickered beside her.

"Don't start this again," Chris snapped.

"Oh, but when *you* start something, it's always allowed?" Blake asked incredulously.

Chris huffed and began cursing in Spanish as Blake rolled his eyes.

Kendall chuckled at the pair of them. She actually found it cute when they argued like a married couple. Not only that, but it helped take her mind off the nerves bubbling in her stomach in anticipation of the fight.

The announcer's voice bellowed through the large crowded room and conversations died down.

Kendall's ears numbed until she heard the name of the man she had fallen flat on her face in love with come through the speakers.

"HERE HE IS... THE STRYKER! READY TO STRIKE AGAIN!" the speakers hollered.

Adrenaline flooded her stomach just hearing his name. She scanned the room frantically, trying to spot his red silk robe, but he was nowhere to be seen.

"You better be searching the crowd for me, Princess," Daniel's husky voice sounded behind her.

A knowing smile creased her face and she spun on her heel to face him.

His chiselled chest peeked out from beneath his red robe and he smirked smugly as he gazed down at her.

"I'll search every crowd for you, Stryker," Kendall said, smitten as a kitten.

Daniel took a step towards her.

"Don't be going soft on me now," he said, placing a hand on the back of her head and softly kissing her forehead.

Butterflies erupted in her stomach, as they always did when he touched her.

"Never," she said cheekily.

They gazed into each other's eyes as if they were the only two people on the planet, neither wanting to look away.

"Go knock 'em dead," Kendall said, smirking.

Daniel smiled brightly and Kendall's pulse doubled at the mouth-watering sight.

"Anything for you, Princess," he said amorously, flashing a toothy grin before jogging over to the ring.

The Cheshire-Cat-like smile on Kendall's face didn't fade.

She wasn't sure it ever would.

Not with Daniel in her life.

Thank you for reading

Thank you for making it all the way to the end. I hope you thoroughly enjoyed my writing and loved my characters as much as I do. If you do like my writing, stay tuned for future novels which are fast on the way.

Acknowledgements

First and foremost, I would like to thank my editor, Patricia Walker. Although, to me she's just 'Pat'. It's amazing to me that an esteemed editor and journalist like herself would be willing to channel her expertise into my little romance novel. I couldn't be more grateful for her edits and her endless support. She has been an absolute dream to work with and I feel very privileged to have had this experience with someone so skilled.

And then there's my parents. Who after watching me only narrowly pass my english exams in school, still continued to show me nothing but support in my pursuit of my first publication. They have always taught me that the world is my oyster and I am certain that I would never have even had the idea to start writing my own novel if they hadn't shown me, by example, that you can do anything that you put your mind to.

I also have to give a huge thank you to my best friend, Anthea, for doing the final read and sending me on my way to the publish button with confidence in my skills as a writer. I hope everyone else loves this book as much as she does.

I have been very lucky to have had such positive encouragement from those around me from the moment I announced my plans to self publish.

Thank you to everyone who gave this book a read. You mean more to me than you will ever know.

Lastly, thank you to Maryna Arsenieva for this gorgeous cover design.

Printed in Great Britain
by Amazon

38441163R00145